The loss of control was dangerous, because the woman who had instigated this kiss was in his employ.

Kate worked for him. Marco had crossed a line and didn't even bother rationalizing it because it was a waste of energy. Instead, he went into damage control mode. *It wouldn't happen again*, he told himself. The few extra feet of physical distance he created seemed a sensible backup plan.

When she spoke, he registered she sounded dazed, appalled even. "Did I start that?"

Could her action have been construed as an invitation to whatever was supposed to follow? She had no words to describe the kiss. She hadn't known a kiss could feel like that, that she could feel want and need in her bones and skin, right to the soles of her feet.

"Yes, but I finished it, and it is..." he said, his steely eyes seeking and finding hers, "...finished."

He said it for his benefit as much as hers.

Kim Lawrence lives on a farm in Anglesey with her university-lecturer husband, assorted pets who arrived as strays and never left, and sometimes one or both of her boomerang sons. When she's not writing, she loves to be outdoors gardening or walking on one of the beaches for which the island is famous—along with being the place where Prince William and Catherine made their first home!

Books by Kim Lawrence

Harlequin Presents

A Passionate Night with the Greek
Claimed by Her Greek Boss

Jet-Set Billionaires

Innocent in the Sicilian's Palazzo

Spanish Secret Heirs

The Spaniard's Surprise Love-Child
Claiming His Unknown Son

A Ring from a Billionaire

Waking Up in His Royal Bed
The Italian's Bride on Paper

Visit the Author Profile page
at Harlequin.com for more titles.

Kim Lawrence

THE PRINCE'S FORBIDDEN CINDERELLA

HARLEQUIN®
PRESENTS™

Recycling programs
for this product may
not exist in your area.

ISBN-13: 978-1-335-58424-3

The Prince's Forbidden Cinderella

Copyright © 2023 by Kim Lawrence

For questions and comments about the quality of this book, please contact us at CustomerService@Harlequin.com.

Harlequin Enterprises ULC
22 Adelaide St. West, 41st Floor
Toronto, Ontario M5H 4E3, Canada
www.Harlequin.com

Printed in U.S.A.

THE PRINCE'S
FORBIDDEN CINDERELLA

For Sally, who dedicated her birthday to raising money for a cause close to my heart. Thank you!

CHAPTER ONE

RENZOI WAS OFTEN referred to as a jewel, and it was rare for those enjoying their first glimpse of the island kingdom from the air to disagree.

There was one airport on the island, and the coastal route from the international airport hub to the walled city capital of Fort St Boniface was considered by many to be one of the most beautiful stretches of road in the world, beloved by film crews over the years, and by those with a head for heights, the nerves for hairpin bends, and a love of dramatic seascapes.

Many travellers who arrived on the island took the less dizzying option of a transfer on one of the water taxis that ferried their passengers across the glittering waters of the grand harbour.

You could no longer gawp at the luxury yachts moored in the deep water as they were now floating, with their billionaire occupants, in a brand-new purpose-built marina on the opposite side of the island, contributing to the island's thriving economy and reputation as a haunt for the rich and famous.

These days the only obstacles to negotiate on the short crossing were a few sailing and fishing boats. Part of the charm of St Boniface was that it remained a working harbour.

The short crossing offered the best view of the walled capital with its towers and domes. Dramatic though the capital's architecture was, it was the royal palace centrepiece, rising like the top tier of a wedding cake above the medieval sprawl of picturesque narrow streets and cobbled squares, that everyone wanted to be snapped outside.

In daylight hours the sparkling stretch of water swarmed with brightly painted speedboats. Even as the sun was replaced by stars and a full moon, several continued to work the stretch, ferrying groups of eager tourists staring with wonder at the illuminated fairytale castle with its dramatic dome and myriad towers.

One such vessel held no tourists, it was not draped with colourful bunting, instead, it carried a solitary passenger and, for the observant, a discreet royal logo illuminated by the strings of twinkling fairy lights reflecting off the water as it reversed towards a pontoon that was set a little away from the main landing area where the tourist fleet was moored.

Seemingly not having the patience to wait for the final manoeuvre, the passenger leapt casually out over the several feet of water and landed with athletic jungle-cat grace on the gently swaying pontoon.

A figure who had been standing on the dock lifted a hand in greeting, pausing as the tall, loose-limbed, suited figure negotiated his way over the pontoon towards him.

'I wasn't expecting a reception party—' the arrival began, only to pause as the phone in his pocket began to vibrate. He raised an apologetic hand. 'One moment, Rafe.'

The waiting figure, who might have been considered tall himself had he not been standing beside the Prince, who stood six four in his bare feet, watched as a spasm of irritated comprehension moved like a slow ripple across the contours of the handsome carved features of the heir to the throne of Renzoi, before the silver-grey eyes lifted to make contact with his.

'I was about to ask if there was a problem, but...' Marco glanced at the screen of his phone one last time before he slid it back into his pocket. 'The airport is closed...?'

The other man gave a rueful nod. 'Everything is grounded. This storm is heading straight for us.'

'You're heading out there now?'

'It kind of comes with the job description.'

'There is a job description for Minister for Transport and Tourism?' Marco drawled, his darkly delineated brows lifting.

The other man gave a self-conscious shrug. 'When someone says "Minister" I keep looking over my shoulder.'

'Not such a bad idea, palace politics being what they are,' Marco observed sardonically. 'Though luckily the knives are *mostly* metaphorical these days. So, how many times have you been told you have big shoes to fill so far?'

'Everyone seems shocked. The minister's death was—'

'Shocked? The man was ninety,' Marco cut in. 'Drank like a fish and the *big* shoes he died in were golf shoes. As his assistant you've already been doing his job for the last five years while he took the accolades.'

Rafe permitted himself a grin, which faded as he added earnestly, 'You putting your neck on the line for me…it meant a lot to me.'

'Neck?' Marco rotated the part of his anatomy under discussion, releasing some of the tension that he hadn't been aware was there.

'Hardly that. You have nothing to prove to me, Rafe.'

His neck was safe but when he had used his veto to override the Council of Ministers' choice to fill the senior vacancy, Marco had known that any mistakes on Rafe's part would be eagerly pounced on as evidence of Marco's meddling in matters he did not understand by the palace mandarins, who preferred he should emulate his much more compliant father.

Nepotism in the palace was an accepted route of promotion. Just five families held virtually every position of power on the island, and they had no intention of ceding that power without a struggle. This was fine, Marco could be patient, and he had his father's backing, even though the King was too easy-going and, yes, it was true, *lazy*, Marco acknowledged, one corner of his mouth lifting in an affectionate grin as he thought of his father, who, as the courtiers pointed out, was much loved by his people.

The hardly subtle shorthand being that if Marco took up golf or beekeeping or taking afternoon tea with his long-term mistress, and left the mandarins to run the country, he too would one day be loved by his people.

Marco, whose marriage had ended with the death of his wife, did not have a long-term mistress, nor a short-term one. He wasn't a monk. One-night or occasionally discreet two-night stands seemed a much less demanding way to satisfy his natural physical needs. Also the old adage that there was safety in numbers held true.

One day he would marry again, but he intended to delay that day for as long as possible.

'At least you made it home before the closures, Highness...'

'*Highness...?* Rafe...*really?*' Marco's expressive lips twitched.

The other man grinned and pushed his wire-framed glasses up his nose. 'All right, Marco, but...'

'*But* there is no one around to hear. You can grovel as much as you like in company, but being called *Highness* by a man I once saw dance on a table after half a cider—you really are a lightweight—and a man I used to thrash at rugby doesn't sit right.' Not that friendship, or even the pleasure of winding up the cabal of blue bloods that took their power for granted, was the reason that Marco had given his old university friend and son of his chauffeur the lynchpin role. It was for the simple reason that Rafe was the best man for the job.

'Rugby... I think recollections may vary on

that one, but as you're my boss I'll let it pass. I take it the flight in was...*interesting*?'

Marco's grin flashed. 'You could say that. I think I have had my week's adrenaline rush.' Had he not known the service history of the decorated pilot at the controls he might have been worried at their third attempt at landing. His grin faded as he observed Rafe's glance drifting to the waiting boat.

'You need to be off?'

Rafe nodded and, excusing himself, climbed into the boat with more caution than Marco had exited it. Marco watched the boat speed away before striding towards the waiting car. As he reached the long, low, armour-plated limo with the blacked-out windows a power surge caused the lights, including those dancing on the water, to flicker.

The door was opened by a suited figure who had emerged from the driver's seat. 'Did you see Rafe, Tomas?'

'My son, the minister,' he self-corrected, 'is working.' Despite the stony expression Marco could hear the pride in the older man's voice.

'Of course.' Marco's finger traced the white scar on his cheek. Tomas had been Marco's personal childhood bodyguard before an injury acquired rescuing Marco after he tested out his youthful theory that a waterfall was made for leaping into and sliding down had put Tomas on desk duty.

The thin white line on his cheek was Marco's only lasting reminder. Tomas's reminder was the bleep of metal detectors when he walked through them, and a limp that had negated his role as a personal security guard.

Desk duty had not suited him, nor had early retirement. He had jumped at the chance to enter service as Marco's personal driver.

'He is grateful for the chance you have given him, Highness.'

'He deserves it.'

'Yes,' the older man agreed factually, adding, 'The storm has followed you home, I think, Highness.'

Marco made a non-committal sound in his throat. He did not assign human characteristics to forces of nature, he simply respected them. The door closed behind him. The air-conditioned interior of the car was pleasant after the sultry pre-storm heaviness outside. Marco loosened his tie and shrugged off his jacket, dislodging the small gift-wrapped package in his breast pocket. It was hard to know what to get a five-year-old girl who had pretty much everything. In the end he'd opted for a delicate necklace, a silver hand-beaten shell on a silver chain.

Would Freya like it?

He had no idea; he dodged the acknowledgment of his ignorance but not before he experienced a stab of something that felt like loss… what five-year-old was *not* a mystery?

Freya would smile and say thank you. His daughter was a very polite child…her old-fashioned manners were a credit to Nanny Maeve, his own nanny back in the day, who was reluctantly retiring due to crippling arthritis, but she had insisted she was well enough to stay on another month and ensure a smooth transition before she moved to the luxurious surroundings of an upmarket retirement village in her native Ireland.

Opening his laptop, he began scrolling through emails as the car drew away from the dock. They had driven through the gate cut into the sixteenth-century walls of the capital before the dark outside was briefly illuminated by a sodium-silver flash that for a brief moment blinded the passenger to the iconic image of the castle. A moment later the much-replicated image of the illuminated honeyed walls that inevitably drew gasps of amazement reappeared.

Marco didn't gasp. He was focusing on the laptop in front of him. He had grown up inside those fortified walls and was more interested in the results of the latest opinion poll he had recently set in motion.

A quick scan of the table of figures twitched the corners of his wide sensual mouth upwards into a satisfied smile. This information would be useful ammunition at tomorrow's scheduled meeting. It was just what he needed to pull the rug from under the expensively shod feet of the cabal of palace officials who held strong to the belief that any change was a bad one.

There were days, in fact entire weeks, when it felt to Marco he was banging his head against a brick wall when he tried to convince the courtiers who felt it was their job to keep the status quo that stagnation was not a good thing, and that the subjects of the admittedly prosperous island state were a lot more open-minded than the courtiers believed.

And the figures he was looking at backed up this view. A representative cross section of the island kingdom's population, when asked their views on a fictional scenario equivalent to the real one he had in mind, were not so closed-minded.

As he closed the laptop the time in the corner of the screen caught his eye, causing him to self-correct the thought. It actually already was tomorrow.

Ahead the gilded gates silently swung open. There was no visible security presence beyond the sentinel figures in traditional dress who stood at intervals along the battlements, but it was there. Marco had signed off on the new improved security measures six months ago in direct response to the *incident* that had involved a tourist armed with nothing more sinister than a camera who had somehow wandered into Freya's fifth birthday party.

A guest speaker at a European climate-change conference, Marco had learnt of the incident second-hand from his mother, who had told it as an amusing anecdote, which was possibly to be expected of a monarch who regularly rode around the island on a bicycle with her security detail trying to keep up.

His mother refused to accept that there were bad people out there…just misunderstood souls. He was surprised her good nature was not taken advantage of more.

Marco had *not* been amused and had instigated a full-scale overhaul of the palace security arrangements. He had not kept her mother safe but the child she had died giving life to would be protected.

Marco pushed away the image of his late wife's pale sweat-slicked face as, utterly exhausted by the traumatic birth, she had refused to look at her newborn child, before the image could shift, as it inevitably did, to the next scene.

The scene that culminated in him standing in front of an empty bed covered in crumpled blood-stained sheets. He always remembered the weight and warmth of the baby in his arms, her big accusing blue eyes looking up at him, before she was whisked away and the doctor appeared, the news he was there to break written in his compassionate eyes.

The weight of the crushing guilt Marco felt at that moment had never lessened. It was always with him. He wore it like a second skin. It was no more than he deserved.

Like his own father, he had failed as a husband. It seemed inevitable that, like his own father, one day he would also fail as a father. To be on the receiving end of his daughter's love would make him feel like the fraud that he was, not the grieving loving husband the world thought of him as.

Was he even capable of loving?

The self-contemptuous curl of his lip flattened as his assistant appeared. 'Luca.'

The young man, knowing his boss's impatience with small talk, fell into step with him and launched straight into the requested update without preamble as the two men walked together towards the entrance of Marco's personal apartments.

They reached the pillared doorway. 'So, the new nanny has arrived?' It was an afterthought.

There was the faintest of pauses before the younger man responded. Marco noted and filed away the information. 'Her flight was delayed, but yes, she's here.'

'But?'

'But I'm afraid the anticipated handover won't be happening. Miss Fitzgerald's sister has been admitted to hospital back home.'

'So where is nanny now?'

'Which one…? Oh, I see… Miss Fitzgerald is in Cork. I put her on a private jet…arranged for someone to meet her on the other end and escort her. Oh, and I sent some flowers to the hospital for her sister… I assumed that you would want…?'

'Of course.' Marco dismissed the unnecessary question with a flick of the long fingers of his left hand, light catching the gold wedding ring he still wore.

So the new nanny would be thrown in at the deep end. He shrugged. He hadn't interviewed her personally but on paper she'd been the best candidate by far—an experienced teacher who had been deputy head in a school of five hundred could look after one small five-year-old. And if she didn't make the grade, the solution was not a difficult one.

Her six-month trial could be terminated at any point and there was a small army of nursery nurses who had learned their trade under nanny Fitzgerald who could fill the gap. He did not foresee a problem, so he moved on to the next issue.

'Luca, could you send over the details of the eco-friendly start-ups who applied for the new sponsorship fund?' Before becoming a father, investing in firms that were intended to address some of the world's environmental challenges would not have been on Marco's radar, but now he was passionate about making the planet's future a safe one for his daughter.

'I already have. There has been quite a response, even after the business team filtered them for obvious duds, though I shouldn't really be surprised. The kudos of having your name and "royal" associated does bring the sort of brand awareness that any start-up—sorry,' he tacked on, stifling a yawn.

Marco felt his guilt stir. *He had to be hell to work for.* Just because he could not manage more than four hours' sleep it didn't mean his staff couldn't have a life outside the office.

'Take tomorrow off.'

The younger man looked startled. 'Oh, but the—'

Marco shook his head, the smile staying in his grey eyes and not altering the sensual line of his firm lips as he reiterated firmly, 'Go home, Luca, and thanks.'

The startled look again and Marco made a note to self to express gratitude where it was due more often. Luca was a really excellent aide and he would be sad to let him go, but the young man had outgrown his position long ago. He deserved some autonomy. The post Marco had in mind for him would give him that.

His own rooms were on the ground floor, his bedroom opening directly to a private quadrangle. Two floors above him was the tower room that he had had equipped as a private gym. Very useful for an insomniac. Choosing between his bed and the treadmill, he selected neither. Instead, he entered the hallway where the stairs led up to the nursery wing.

The need to see his daughter was a physical ache. She would be sleeping but she often was when he chose to visit her. It was easier than when she was awake. Pain flickered across the strong contours of his face. Her eyes were so like her mother's, the woman he had not loved.

Her eyes accustomed to the dark now, Kate looked around the unfamiliar room and the unfamiliar objects from her position in the high canopied four-poster.

She was really here, and in the process of getting here she had burnt all her bridges. Her stomach tightened as she was seized by a deep visceral longing for all things familiar: her tiny home snuggled between an antique shop and a tea room, her classroom… *Stop it, Kate,* she told herself sternly, *look forward not back!*

Her thoughts were slow to react to the reprimand and lingered on the image of her parents' hurt, guilty faces when she had confronted them…

'You lied to me, all my life you lied, my entire life has been a lie. I need to get away.'

They thought she'd been talking about a holiday. Good idea, they'd said, suggesting a week somewhere warm.

Then she'd seen the online ad.

A new job, a new life.

'It's so far away, Kate,' her dad had said.

'We will miss you,' her mum had said.

Kate fought free of the memories. Just because she had stepped off the path she'd been on did not mean, as her brother had claimed, she was punishing Mum and Dad. It was good to get out of your comfort zone, especially if you were trying to get to grips with your life when everything that made you feel safe and who you were had vanished.

Comfort zone, she mused with a wry twist

of her lips as she looked around her surroundings, thinking, *And then some.*

The post had been advertised as live-in and though she hadn't been expecting a room in the attic, given who her employer was, she had been taken aback, pleasantly, when she had arrived at the palace to be shown to a self-contained luxury apartment. Self-contained up to the point there was an adjoining door to the nursery occupied by her new charge, Princess Freya, a shy five-year-old with big blue eyes who she had met very briefly when she had arrived.

Raising herself on one elbow, she reached for her phone and groaned when she saw the time. Every cell in her body was aching from exhaustion but her brain was buzzing. Flopping back down, her flame red hair spread across the silk pillow, she swept back with the crook of her elbow a tangled shiny strand of long golden auburn that was tickling her nose, and sighed before levering herself upright once more and shaking her head to free the fiery strands that were sticking to the dampness of her skin.

Renzoi, she had read during her fact-finding Internet frenzy after she had got the job, enjoyed an enviable temperate climate.

This didn't feel temperate, it felt clammy

and stiflingly hot. Pushing back the covers, she swung her legs out of bed and padded barefoot across to the window and, pulling aside the heavy curtains, she stood on tiptoe to unfasten the window latch and settled back on her heels as the warm air rushed in. At least the light breeze was welcome. She pulled at the neck of her loose cotton nightgown and, head back, she breathed, lifting her hair from her neck to give the breeze access to her hot sticky skin. Her nostrils flared as the room was filled with the strong night-time scents redolent of mint and rosemary. Her reading matter had told her that both grew wild on the hills of the island.

She wandered out of the bedroom and through the pretty living room, into the fitted kitchen with its stone worktops. In the morning she would tackle the coffee machine, which looked impossibly complicated. She opened the fridge, which was stocked with an assortment of essentials, and enjoyed the cool as she filled her glass with iced water from the dispenser.

As she gulped down the water she caught sight of her reflection in one of the shiny cupboards. She looked like a pale wraith, a ghostly vision in need of a comb, some concealer for the dark shadows under her eyes and a good meal. Not that the meal part would matter—

no matter *what* she ate her collarbones stood out, leaving delicate hollows above. She envied other women their lush curves, not that her lack of them kept her awake nights.

She was firmly of the mind that you worked with what you had. From nowhere the tears welled in her eyes, emotion kept locked inside spilling out in the form of salty liquid that slid down her cheeks.

She gave a loud sniff. 'Oh, God, Kate, what are you doing?'

Running away? Trying to find herself?

Her lips twisted in a grimace of self-mockery. A few weeks earlier she would have poured scorn on both options. She was proud that she never avoided reality even when it was not palatable.

Take her early obsession with ballet, not in itself so unusual for a young girl, but what set her apart was the fact she didn't drift away like most of her friends and become distracted by the latest craze or boys. The only thing that had made her walk away from her dream was the realisation that she lacked the indefinable *something* that a top-class dancer needed. She would only ever be competent.

Competent wasn't good enough, the brutal truth was her best wasn't good enough, so she had diverted her passion into something that she didn't have to be second-best at: her schoolwork. And then, after she won a scholarship to a top university, gaining a degree in teaching.

Kate knew she was a good teacher. Her natural aptitude for engaging children's interest and her work ethic had been recognised.

The youngest deputy head at the prestigious primary school, being groomed, everyone knew, to take over when the head retired in two years. Not that she'd necessarily intended to take the post—she'd had a tentative approach from a failing inner-city school in a deprived area. They needed someone with an innovative approach to turn the school around, someone who thrived on a challenge.

She was no longer the person who had been excited by the idea, the person who had known who she was and where she was going. Now, shaking her head and brushing the last cooling tear from her face, she closed the fridge door.

Bed, she decided, calculating that if she fell asleep in the next thirty minutes she could still get five hours' sleep in before she had to get up again.

She had barely taken a couple of steps when a sound made her pause. Head tilted to one side, she listened, straining to make it out. *Music?* Her brow furrowed. Or a *voice*?

There was nothing but silence. She shrugged. She had imagined it. A few moments later, her hand reaching for the handle of her bedroom door, she stopped. This time there was no doubt: another noise, a thump and even a muffled curse, emanating from the speaker on the wall that, as had been explained to her earlier, was wired into the nursery. It was one piece of the massive amount of information she had received that her time-zone-whacked brain had retained.

It was not the sort of sound a child made... it was...

There was someone in Freya's room and the only way to find out who was to go in. She stared, her thoughts racing, at the wall that separated the room from the nursery, seeing the layout in her head, rows of books, their spines colour-coordinated, educational toys and...well, actually it looked like a very expensive toy store glossy advert. Everything looked pristine, brand new, neatly arranged on shelves and in labelled boxes. A world away from her own childhood bedroom or, for that matter, her brother's.

Thinking of her brother brought a half-smile to her face. It lasted a split second before she remembered the row they'd had before she left.

Like she would ever forget? The spark left her eyes as the sense of betrayal resurfaced.

It had been enough of a life-changing blow to learn that her parents, who had always taught her the importance of truth and honesty in life, had been lying to her, but discovering that her brother had been party to the conspiracy of deceit had been worse somehow.

She would never forget the expression she'd seen in his eyes when she had broken it to him, but before he'd said a word she'd known that this was not news to him.

He'd known they were adopted, that he wasn't even her brother.

They had argued before but nothing like the argument that had followed. Jake, she'd discovered, had found out by accident too, but years ago and he couldn't see why she had a problem.

'It doesn't change anything.'

For Kate it changed *everything.* She really couldn't understand *how* he could feel that way. Jake told her that this reaction was exactly why he hadn't told her.

She dashed away a stray tear angrily as the conversation ran through her head.

'You're the best friend, or sister, a person could have. You'd fight to the death for the people you love.'

'And that is a bad thing?'

'You don't just love Mum and Dad, you put them on a pedestal, Kate. You're tough on yourself and the rest of us, you expect too much. Can't you see that Mum and Dad were protecting you, I was protecting you?'

'You don't protect someone from the truth.'

He had not even come to say goodbye.

Kate gave her head an angry little shake to dislodge the memories and thought, *Stop dithering.* Straightening her narrow shoulders, she pulled the connecting door open. Whatever was on the other side could not be more disturbing than the company of her own thoughts.

Or maybe not?

CHAPTER TWO

DESPITE HER THUDDING HEART, Kate did not actually expect to discover anything sinister on
the other side of the door and she was fully
prepared to feel stupid.

In her head she was inventing crazy scenar-
ios she'd discover, the room filled with people
disinfecting the toys, or sweeping for bugs, the
snooping kind, or maybe both…? The nursery
did not remain showroom pristine without a
lot of work.

So, it took Kate several frozen seconds before the adrenaline rush kicked into life. By
this point the large figure on the opposite side
of the room had put a toy doll back on a shelf
that was, her racing brain noted irrelevantly,
out of reach to a five-year-old. For that matter
it was out of reach for someone her own height,
which was a diminutive five three.

It was definitely *not* out of reach for the intruder, whose back view was revealed by the

light shining from the room behind her as tall and also powerful. She took in the stretch of fabric across his shoulders, making her aware of the muscles beneath the tailoring. This was one well-dressed and very fit intruder!

If good tailoring was an indicator of character, she had nothing to worry about, but it wasn't, and she did.

Better to assume the worst and laugh when the innocent truth was revealed, but laughter would be premature. The main thing was to stay calm and not panic...

Oh, God, the panic button beside her bed!

Five minutes ago was the time to remember that. When the red button had been pointed out to her it had seemed a massive overkill because you'd need to be some sort of ninja warrior or possess superpowers to get past the armed guards that had seemed to be lurking around every corner during her whirlwind tour of the nursery wing.

The point was someone had, and the button was not within reach. She weighed the option of retreating but realised the chances of doing so without alerting this man to her presence were zero. He was going to turn around any second, at which point she might discover there was a perfectly reasonable explanation for him being there, but she wasn't about to give him the benefit of the doubt. Caution was called for and there was a five-year-old child to think about.

He'd have to go through her to get to her new charge… *Which probably wouldn't take more than a few seconds.* She pushed the unhelpful thought away and, her bare feet silent on the polished boards—not so her heart, which was throwing itself against her ribcage—she edged towards the little princess's bedroom door. The intruder remained oblivious to her presence.

She reached the door, took her position and cleared her throat, trying to project her inner Amazonian kick-boxer, while aware that on the outside what he would see made any threat she made laughable.

'Security is on its way.' Pleased her voice did not even wobble, she pushed ahead with her warning. 'I suggest you—'

'Hold on a moment, will you?' Marco pushed out between gritted teeth, irritated that the entire elaborate toy display was about to slide once more, domino fashion, off the shelf. On the plus side, the new nanny possessed not only a pleasant speaking voice but excellent hearing, which was one up on her predecessor, who'd refused to wear the hearing aids she really had needed in her advancing years. It could make for some interesting conversations, especially as she took offence if you raised your voice.

She squeaked when one of the dolls let out a horribly realistic crying sound. Marco's response was to swear, proving he had mastered three languages or at least he knew how to swear multilingually.

'Right, sorry about that.' Marco turned, transferring his attention towards the waiting new nanny…only to discover that the person standing there was *not* the new nanny!

He refused to accept this possibility as for a few stark mind-freezing seconds his brain shut down. Not so his primal functions. Hormones pumped through his bloodstream, leaving heat that pooled hot and heavy in his groin and making a mockery of both the control he prided himself on and his much-admired lightning wits.

In two startled blinks he took in the cause of the blip in his self-control, his glance sweeping her from head to toe—not a long journey. She was petite.

He knew about female nightwear. He'd removed quite a bit of it over the years, but none that looked like the thing the woman standing there was wearing. Not intended to titillate or light the sort of fire it had in him and therein lay the irony. The white cotton shapeless thing covered quite a lot and heavily hinted at a hell of a lot more, courtesy of the directional beam of the wall light in the adjoining flat making it one shade short of transparent. It revealed the dark tips of her small high breasts, the dip and flare at her waist and hip and the shadow at the juncture of the slim, sinuous length of her thighs.

Her skin was the next pale on the colour spectrum to her nightdress but, unlike the fabric, had a pearly, almost opalescent quality. Again, probably courtesy of the lighting. She possessed the most extraordinary hair he'd ever seen; the lustrous waves and heavy coils didn't need any lighting effects to reveal the gold highlight interwoven with the deep titian waves that fell untidily around her small oval face and tumbled down her back.

As their glances connected her luminous amber eyes widened and her mouth fell, not unattractively, open. As he stared at the pink, slightly quivering outline any number of inappropriate thoughts slithered through his mind. Inappropriate when thought in connection with his daughter's nanny and they made it hard to retain his mental image of the anticipated sensible female in his head. In essence she would be a slightly younger version of Nanny Maeve, all no-nonsense common sense and even more sensible shoes. His glance ran to her bare narrow feet and glittery painted toenails.

Clearing his throat, he dragged his gaze upwards.

'If you're not going to use that...?' He nodded at the porcelain vase she held in a white-knuckled grip.

He watched her eyes travel to the ugly thing in her hand, a look of surprise widening the eyes she took off him for one split second. Her elbow dropped but not all the way, similarly her defences as she retained a grip of both.

'Your only chance of braining me was utilising the element of surprise and you've lost that now, so you might as well put it down.'

Tomorrow, he decided grimly, he was going to find out which proxy had decided at interview that this woman represented a suitably *mature* candidate. And it wouldn't have been one person; the vetting procedure would have been as detailed as the background check.

Deep velvet with an edge of gravel to the dark chocolate flavour, his sardonic drawl shook Kate free of the thrall that had held her staring transfixed, mouth open, drooling... She closed her mouth with a snap.

Drooling...? God, I really hope not.

'You could drop it if you like. It'll be insured and it is extremely ugly.'

With elaborate care she placed the vase she didn't actually recall picking up in a space beside a row of colour-coded books that she already had marked out as one of her first changes.

As first impressions went it was hard to imagine one worse than this. 'S-Sorry...' she stuttered and stopped.

What was she meant to call him?

'I didn't realise it was Your...' *Highness? Majesty?*

Obviously, she knew *who* he was. Crown Prince Marco—then a lot of other names followed—Zanetti, her new boss. His every utterance was picked up across the media spectrum, analysed to the nth degree and imbued with hidden, deep meaning.

His height and his superb athletic body meant that a photo of him shirtless, all golden skin and sculpted muscle, was worth mega bucks. Even an image of him conservatively dressed in a suit could send social media wild, especially as they were relatively rare. His face with its razor-sharp cheekbones, silver-grey stare and sinfully sexy mouth had been called perfect, though now she was seeing it in the flesh she decided she agreed with one jaundiced critic who had called it *too* perfect!

For the first twelve months after his beautiful wife's tragic death in childbirth, he'd vanished, fallen off the edge of the earth. One or two snaps of him looking brooding and beautiful in a hollow-eyed, gaunt-faced way had been the only visuals to feed the appetite for news about the iconic tragic figure he had become in the eyes of the world.

Does a man ever recover from the loss of his first love?

Learning to love again...will Marco?

Advice from someone who has been there and come out the other side.

Is Marco putting his child ahead of his happiness?

Hypnosis and a carb-free diet helped me recover from PTSD after my boyfriend left me, it could help the lonely Prince too.

The headlines, from the inane to the academic, all had a similar theme, and who knew? Maybe the man under discussion read them, because the tragic prince did move on.

A year after his wife's death Marco Zanetti re-emerged, affording an interested public discreet glimpses of his private life. His name started to be linked with a succession of beautiful women. The longevity of his associations with the women he escorted varied, one night or a week—this was presumably his version of long-term.

No matter how discreet or short-lived the liaisons were, inevitably every beautiful woman his name was linked with was viewed as a prospective future queen and mother, her privacy invaded, her past love life scrutinised. Despite this price, which to Kate, whose blood ran cold at the thought, seemed a high one, there was no shortage of candidates, which had seemed inexplicable, though less so now when she was standing in the same room as him.

Luckily he was a million miles from the sort of man she found attractive—her type was good-looking, but not too good-looking, kind and sensitive. Shaking her head slightly to clear it, she tried to kick-start her brain for the correct form of address.

It was so damned frustrating. She'd made a point of knowing, and the knowledge had simply fled. Maybe because worrying about titles offended her egalitarian nature?

She had already decided that she would not be curtseying to anyone.

She finally settled for a slightly breathless, 'Freya's dad, that is you, or... I heard a noise and—'

Marco cut across her before she ran out of steam. 'And you are...?'

The Prince sounded haughty and looked... well, he looked like something out of a fan-

tasy—or a nightmare, depending on your pref-
erences, and her fantasies were *not* of men with
hauteur stamped into their too handsome features, even if he really was several billion
times more dramatically gorgeous in the flesh
than in print or video.

The camera made him look good, it accurately
captured his patrician features, all hard angles
and intriguing carved hollows, the tummy-quiv-
ering gleam in his heavy-lidded silver-grey eyes
with the famous long lashes, his masterful nose
and the much-raved-about sexy mouth.

Kate had always privately suspected that the
real in-the-flesh man would be a bit of a let-
down. She'd been prepared for it. What she
hadn't been ready for was the fact that no photo
could do him justice. It did not even hint at the
skin-peelingly raw masculinity he exuded or his
physical presence so strong it seemed to suck
the oxygen from the room, or at least her lungs.

Her chin lifted as she tried to regain a little
dignity. As first impressions went…maybe he
had a sense of humour but, looking at his fallen-
angel dark face, she decided it was doubtful.

'I'm Kate Armstrong, the new nanny.'

She took a step forward and held out her
hand, dropping it a couple of humiliating moments later when he showed no sign of taking it.

God, perhaps it was against the law to touch his royal personage.

'Should I curtsey?' The words were out before she could stop them.

Marco's eyes slid to the high but loose neckline of her nightdress. His eyes darkened a shade to steel.

'Probably not.'

The way his eyes slid downwards made Kate remember for the first time that she was just in her nightdress. The knowledge that it was the sort of nightdress your grandmother would approve of eased her flurry of sink-through-the-floor horror.

'I appreciate your efforts to protect Freya, but the next time maybe just press the panic button...?' The sardonic suggestion sent the heat flying back to her cheeks. She resented the fact he could make her feel a total idiot just by lifting one of his eyebrows.

'Oh, gosh, yes, definitely,' she agreed, nodding her agreement and vowing there would not be a next time. She wouldn't give the sarcastic superior devil the satisfaction to patronise her. 'But I wasn't in bed. I couldn't sleep, it's so hot.'

She pulled at the neck of her nightdress, seemingly oblivious to the provocativeness of the action.

'A storm is coming,' Marco said, feeling the prickles of attraction like a rash across his overheated flesh as he dragged his glance upwards, only to have it fall on her soft sensual mouth with the promise of… He brought his line of speculation to an abrupt control-claiming halt.

This was crazy. There were any number of attractive women working at the palace, which proudly proclaimed itself an equal opportunities employer, but it was irrelevant to Marco. There was a code—which his father had never quite got his head around—which meant that there were things a man in his position did not do, and that was sleep with a woman who called him Highness, or sir, or, in this case, *Freya's dad*.

The fact was his annoyance was not about her uncontrollable flamelike hair or her sensual mouth, or the sledgehammer attraction hit her appearance had delivered. It was the fact that she was wrong for the job, too young, too much of a temptation for staff less controlled than he was. He wanted a calming, stable influence for his daughter, he told himself, choosing to forget the occasions recently when his daughter's lack of spontaneity and mischief had caused him the occasional passing concern, enough concern for him to ask his mother's opinion.

'Freya is a sweet little thing. We have lovely cosy chats. She is not the least bit like you. I never had a moment's peace worrying about what you'd do next.'

Her response had eased his concerns, even though his mother had not to his knowledge ever worried about his welfare. That arduous task had been delegated to nanny. Pretty well nothing disturbed his parent's serenity, which as far as he could tell was achieved by deciding that she simply wouldn't see or hear anything that wasn't *nice*, including her husband's in-house mistress.

Kate shivered. She had never liked storms much, though she wondered if the electricity she felt in the air was entirely to do with atmospheric conditions and was not connected in some small way to the gleam in his slitted sliver eyes.

'How long is your trial for, Miss Armstrong?' he asked.

Kate, who had been surreptitiously edging towards the door, froze at the abrupt question. *'Trial?'* She looked at him, her nose wrinkling as she focused, or tried to. This had been a long day that had been topped by making a total fool of herself in front of her new boss. She expelled a slow steadying breath. She'd seen the clause in her contract but had not really paid it much notice.

'Six months...oh...' Comprehension dawned. 'I do know how important continuity is for a child,' she told him earnestly. 'I would never leave you in the lurch,' she went on to assure him, sounding shocked at the idea of such dereliction of duty. 'I'm yours until Freya starts school formally.' Seven seemed late to Kate, but, as the educational system on the island was envied around the world, she was willing to learn. In fact, she was eager.

'You are mine,' Marco mocked and was punished for his cruelty, or rewarded, depending on your viewpoint, by a rush of hormonal heat. This was more than slightly insane. He had gone too long without.

It was an obvious explanation for this explosion of unprecedented lust. His recent work-pleasure balance had of late been pretty heavily skewed in favour of work. He needed to make the effort, though that was part of the problem. There was no effort.

He knew most women he was attracted to would be available, not because of his irresistible charm, but because of who he was, and if he was honest the entire *effort* involved in the mating ritual had become…tiresome. Boredom had set in. It was all so predictable, as was the inevitable post-coital guilt that followed those moments of mind-blanking pleasure when he forgot, when he lost himself in sex. No matter how mind-blowing the sex was, he paid the price in guilt, the *empty* feeling.

Kate watched the Prince rub the gold marriage band on his finger with his thumb, a reminder of what he'd lost, but it didn't make his mockery any more palatable or this situation any more comfortable.

'I'm your employee and I'd frankly feel more comfortable discussing my role here during office hours and when I'm not jet-lagged and likely to say something I'll regret.' She registered from the look of astonishment that washed over his face that she probably already had. She was too tired and stressed by the situation to care much. 'Goodnight, and sorry to disturb you… Your…'

There was a sudden loud rumble of thunder, the vibration continuing long after the sound died. It wasn't the only vibration. The sudden shock had made her flinch and drawn a soft cry of shock from her lips. It also affected her centre of gravity. She had the oddest feeling of being drawn towards his mid-section, which looked as solid as iron. Her delicate fingers flexed as she made a conscious effort to re-dress the balance, quite literally.

She'd heard about male magnetism before, but she'd never actually felt the tug person-ally.

She was shaking. Marco could see the fine tremors running through her body. Sympathy overrode the justified irritation he felt towards her having been dropped into his neatly managed life, a small piece that didn't fit and skewed the neat symmetry of the whole.

'You're afraid of storms?' he said, thinking quite weirdly of her soft warm body burrowing into him for comfort. *Burrowing* was a thing he discouraged in women, or he would have if any had shown the desire to do so.

He'd grown to be a good judge of women who wanted sex without the window dressing, which was useful because there were a lot of women who wanted the window dressing, es-pecially a crown. Marco was under no illusions he was the optional extra; it was the status he represented they wanted.

The women he shared a bed with had one thing in common: they were all happy with sex on equal terms. They were discreet and if their lives and careers got a little boost from the media speculation of being seen with him, that seemed fair.

Kate reacted to his sympathy as though he'd just insulted her. 'I am fine with storms,' she lied, accompanying her words with a chin-jutting glare.

At that moment she'd have chopped off a finger and not admitted it hurt. She would not admit to any weakness because she had just discovered a weakness she had not seen coming.

It wasn't on a par with discovering you were adopted, but it still came as bad news to realise that she was susceptible to the waves of hot male magnetism he oozed.

But she was, and the discovery made her feel horribly self-aware, and, yes, vulnerable too. More vulnerable than meeting your boss in a granny nightie could explain away.

This was far worse, far deeper, an awareness of vulnerability of the body that the acres of cotton concealed. She was more aware of her body than she had ever been. She shifted her weight from one foot to the other, conscious of the feeling of congestion low in her pelvis.

It rocked her to her core to have a fresh set of preconceptions challenged, to realise that it actually was possible to lust after someone you really didn't instinctively like. *Liking* was not necessary in an employer-employee relationship and luckily that was the only relationship there was ever going to be here.

'Goodnight.'

Looking at the closed door, he pondered the extraordinary fact that he had just been reprimanded by an employee, but employee didn't seem the right description—this woman clearly had no concept of hierarchy.

CHAPTER THREE

MARCO HAD HOPED his father could be coaxed into showing some interest, but so far his response had been vague at best. Marco pretended not to notice the multiple hints the conversation was over and continued to push his theme.

'You'll agree that primogeniture is outdated…?' he asked, throwing the question over his shoulder as he walked towards the window. 'That a male taking precedence over an older sister is wrong.'

'I'd offer you tea, but—'

'It's fine. I don't want tea.' He resisted the temptation to point out he didn't like tea and had never drunk the stuff in his thirty-two years.

The King sighed and regarded his son with an attitude of resignation. His only child never had been able to take a hint and once he got an idea into his head he was exhaustingly relentless. 'I hear what you are saying, Marco, but is it worth upsetting people?'

'Upsetting?'

His father sighed again. 'The council, you know they won't like it, Marco. They have strong opinions on tradition.'

Marco smiled, biting his tongue to prevent himself saying of how little interest the *council's* opinion was to him and where he would have loved to suggest, politely of course, they could shove their opinions in anatomical detail.

'The opinion poll I put out there shows quite clearly that the public at large won't have a problem with this. The figures—'

The King held out a hand to halt the flow of information. 'If you say so.'

'So you agree in principle, Father, that Freya should be given precedence over any son I might have?'

'Of course. Are you thinking of getting married again, then? That's good…a king *should* be married. Without your mother's support…' The King caught his son's eyes and his voice trailed away.

'I won't be King for many years,' Marco pointed out swiftly. This at least was one decision he could push down the road. 'And when I am you can be sure I will fulfil all my obligations.' He might be considered a maverick by the palace courtiers who worshipped tradition basically because it was good for them, but Marco had been brought up to respect the role he had been born into. He loved and had pride in his country, and he accepted that one day marriage would be necessary.

And when it came there would be no tragic rerun. The next time, his bride would know that while respect, liking and hopefully great sex would be part of their contract, love would not be.

Unless of course he fell in love... A gleam of self-contempt filtered into his heavy-lidded stare as he contemplated this very unlikely possibility.

If that had been going to happen it would have by now. If he were capable of falling in love it would have been with Belle. The guilt hit him as it always did, clutching like an icy fist in his belly when he thought of his dead wife. The woman who had died before she had lived—and the life she'd shared with him had been some sort of half-life.

If she hadn't married him, she would still be alive.

It *should* have worked. They had been friends long before they had become engaged. He'd *liked* her, and surely liking and respect, two people who had similar viewpoints on the important subjects on life, were a more solid basis for marriage than some unrealistic fantasy based on a temporary hormonal reaction.

He remembered when Belle was in her early teens, her own parents had divorced. Both had been members of one of *the* families in Renzoi. It had created a stir in the general populace, and misery for all involved. His own parents had been together but they had fallen out of love and he and Belle had bonded as unhappy teens over the shared experience of parental mess-ups!

She'd been the first to say it... *'When we grow up let's never fall in love, Marco.'*

If you'd never fallen in love, you couldn't fall out of it. The logic of the plan had stayed with him, but Belle had grown up and she had fallen in love—with him. She'd hoped that he would learn to love her, and it had killed her.

It had always been there, the elephant in the room that he had dealt with by ignoring. But that had become impossible when he had found her weeping. Her tearful, 'It's a girl,' had left him bewildered. His awkward attempt to soothe her had resulted in the truth spilling out of her, the hopes she had kept hidden.

She had believed that giving him a male heir would make him love her back. He had told her in all honesty that he didn't care what sex the child was, and that he would always love her as his dearest friend and the mother of his child.

'But you'll never be in love with me, will you, Marco?'

It was the moment that the truth killed something inside her... *Why the hell couldn't he have lied?*

Experiencing an ice-water rush of the toxic shame the memories brought with them, Marco claimed the present, letting his father's voice drag him back to the moment.

'Rosa has been telling me about the new nanny.'

The changes were micro—Marco's lashes veiled his eyes, his shoulders tensed—subtle, but they were there.

Lady Rosa. Her official title was Master of the Royal Household, but her unofficial title was the King's mistress.

The widow of a minor royal, she was responsible for overseeing the domestic and social calendars across the royal residences, a job she carried out with unflappable calm and efficiency. Marco had hated her very existence once, back when he had thought his parents were a happy couple. Now his attitude was far more pragmatic.

'Don't worry about it, I'll sort it,' he cut in, only too easily able to imagine what Rosa had said about the would-be red-headed usurper to the old favourite Nanny Maeve's role.

'Sort...?' The King looked confused. 'Rosa said you have chosen well. That the woman is a breath of fresh air who knows her mind—those were her words, and coming from Rosa that is quite a compliment.'

Marco compressed his lips over a biting retort. Easy-going to a fault, his father was *not* easy when it came to defending his mistress from criticism.

Marco's restraint did not come easily. It had been years in the making. For a large part of his life the mention of his father's mistress had been enough to trigger one of the monumental arguments he'd had with his father during his teens.

The way he had discovered the affair had not helped. Walking in on his father in bed with his mistress, or in this instance on a sofa with her, was one image he really wished even now that he could un-see. Almost more infuriating was the fact his mother tolerated the situation, which she said made her husband *happy*.

The entire set-up encapsulated for him the utter hypocrisy of marriage, the damage that people did in the name of true love and the fact that if he had never been born three people would have been happier.

Nowadays there was a truce. Marco accepted that it was their life. They had found themselves in an imperfect situation and they had made the best of it. If it hadn't been for his unexpected appearance after years of trying for a child, his parents would have quietly divorced with the blessing of the council, who were anti-divorce but could get very flexible when it came to maintaining the continuity of the throne.

It would be small wonder if Rosa resented him. Without him she'd probably be Queen now. Trying to conceive him had put his parents' marriage under strain. *Well, that's life for you,* he thought with an internal shrug as he gathered up the printouts he'd brought for his father knowing the King would not look at them. Glancing at the wafer-thin metallic watch on his wrist, Marco made his excuses, pretending not to notice that his father looked relieved.

After depositing the papers in his own office and responding to a couple of emails, he looked around for Luca and remembered he'd given him the day off in a moment of uncharacteristic generosity.

His movements around the room woke the dog in his basket but he went back to sleep after Marco had found the magic spot behind his ears. He was not as young as he once had been, but then who was? Marco mused, stretching, his expression growing thoughtful as he recalled the *look* he'd noticed from Luca the previous night when the nanny situation had come up. There were two explanations for that: either his assistant didn't want to be the messenger that got shot or he had a thing about the newest employee.

It seemed about time he took charge of the nanny situation personally because so far delegation had gone so well...*not!*

Was he the *only* person in the place who could see the stark staring obviousness? An image of the flame-haired woman drifted across his vision. The woman, despite her impeccable qualifications, was totally unsuitable.

Because you can't stop thinking about how very suitable she would feel under you, Marco mocked the voice in his head.

Reviewing the previous night, Kate filed her part in it under *Could have handled things better*.

She might well have already lost her job before it had started. Not a good look on a CV, but if she was ready to pretend last night had never happened maybe her employer might be also. In her opinion he hadn't come out of it very well either.

Whatever the reality was, she was going to do what she was being paid for, which was not to become obsessed with her boss. Sure, he was good to look at, but didn't he just know it? The uncharitable thought was immediately followed by a slug of shame as she realised she was making this nasty assessment purely on his spectacular looks and the debilitating effect he had on her nervous system.

He might be vain, he might be humble—a *big* if there—but she had no intention of allowing herself to be sucked into the entire tragic past situation, or the length of his crazy eyelashes, or his mouth. *Do not even go there, Kate.* Though in her defence there was no harm in looking, was there?

Good to establish that just in case it turned out she couldn't *not* look.

There was a table in an alcove in the nursery, which Freya had solemnly explained was the quiet reading area. Her husky tones suggested this rule had been quite rigid.

'I cleared my own place after breakfast,' she added proudly.

'So do you always have breakfast here?'

The little girl nodded.

Kate's throat ached with the emotion lodged

there, and nostalgia for her own different break-
fasts when she had been five, the good-natured
and occasionally not so good-natured bickering.
Quiet was one thing they had not been.

Of course, things had changed as she and
Jake had got older. Breakfast had become less
of a social start to the day and more self-ser-
vice, with her mum putting the toast in her
hand and packed lunch in her school bag as
she left to catch the bus, her mother yelling
after her that breakfast was the most important meal of the day.

The wistful wave of sadness and loss was,
for a split second, so intense that she couldn't
breathe.

They might often have been short of cash
but compared to this rich little princess she
had been wealthy.

*And you threw it all away on a stupid stiff-
necked principle!*

Pinning on a smile, she turned a deaf ear
to the troublemaking voice in her head, and
reminded herself that *she* was the one in the
right. They'd all lied to her and then made out
she was the unreasonable one! Well, Jake had,
at least.

'Did you have a nice breakfast?'

'I did,' said Kate, who had located the rather

upper-crust staff dining room with some dif-
ficulty.

Her entrance had drawn a lot of curious
looks, some friendly, some less so. There
had been a faint buzz when she had selected
a table, after recognising one of the nursery
maids she had seen the previous day.

The reason for the buzz became clear when
the young girl looked surprised and explained
that Kate was allowed on one of the other tables. It didn't immediately click, but when she
examined the people sitting on the other table,
the significance of the lack of uniforms and
the preponderance of suits hit her. The tables,
she realised, were actually arranged in order
of hierarchy and apparently in the scheme of
things she was several tables above a mere
nursery maid.

She had laughed and pronounced herself
quite happy where she was. The food might
be Michelin-star stuff but the entire set-up be-
longed, in her opinion, in the Dark Ages.

But then a child eating in the nursery alone
was in itself a brutal Dark Ages throwback.

'Do you eat all your meals here?' Kate
asked, nodding as one of the maids appeared
carrying the tray she had requested earlier.
'Oh, thank you…just put it down there.'

'Oh, no, Granny has me over to lunch quite

often.' The little girl looked at the tray and its contents. 'It's too early for my milk and apple,' she observed anxiously.

Kate responded to the five-going-on-forty-five comment with professional discretion, even though she just wanted to hug the child. 'This is a "saying hello" break to get to know one another. Granny sounds fun.'

'Oh, she is…and Grandpa too. We have picnics, though I get my knees dirty and nanny… the old nanny looked sad. Grandpa says it doesn't matter, he gets messy loads, but he's King so nobody tells him what to do. Papa will be King after him and then my brother, when I have one. He paints, you know, Grandpa.' She lifted a conspiratorial hand to half cover her mouth. 'He's not very good, but Granny says I have to be kind so I say I like them.'

As she listened to the artless confidences it seemed to Kate that the Prince could take some lessons from this interesting-sounding monarch.

'And Daddy…do you eat with him sometimes?'

'Daddy is a very busy man.'

Kate could almost see the invisible quote marks around the sentence. The man, she brooded, was actually even more of an idiot than she had decided he was.

'Nanny says he has very important things on his mind and I shouldn't bother him.'

This extra information sent Kate's temper into double digits. She imagined that Prince Marco's mind was most often focused on which six-foot model to bed next, if his reputation was to be believed! Keeping her opinion of a man who was *far too busy* for his own daughter to herself, she managed a smile despite wanting to hit something or, more accurately, *someone*.

'Well, I have our special early elevenses on my mind so do you think someone could fetch me a chair so I can join you?'

'All you have to do is ring and you can have anything you want.'

That had to be the saddest sentence she had ever heard, Kate reflected as she sat on her requested chair, which had magically appeared in seconds. What this child needed no *ring* was going to give her. What she needed was a daddy who cared!

The second chair was identical to the one that was the perfect size for Freya. The fit on her was comical enough to make the child giggle before she put her hand over her mouth to smother the sound, as if she expected to be reprimanded.

'Do you think I'll break it?' Kate asked as

she balanced on the seat, feeling glad for the sake of her modesty she had opted to wear a pair of pale blue linen culottes with a darker blue sleeveless silk blouse that she wore tucked into the plaited belt. She hoped the outfit gave the professional but practical look she had been aiming for.

Her stint with an infant class had taught her that you needed to stay flexible and not just physically. A young mind not weighed down by preconceptions could seriously challenge you. She had always liked that part of working with young children.

The smile crept back on the little girl's face. 'Don't worry if you do, I'll say I did it. No one will shout at me, they'll just be disappointed.'

This heartbreaking statement did not give Kate a good opinion of her predecessor or, for that matter, the child's father. In her mind he already had a set of horns, now he had added the forked tail to match.

It had always made sense to her that the devil would be handsome—how else would he make sin look tempting? She could imagine that Marco Zanetti could make sin look *very* attractive.

'Are you hot?' Freya asked innocently.

Taking control of her wilful imagination, Kate called a halt to the speculative stream of steamy images sliding through her head under the title of sin and Marco and willed the guilty colour in her cheeks to fade.

'No, not really, and I won't break the chair, Freya, so don't worry. I'm actually quite skinny. My brother says my hair weighs more than I do.' Her smile faded and her hair came in handy as a distraction as she tossed her ponytail over her shoulder as she swallowed past the lump in her throat. 'How about you pull up your chair and we have some cake to celebrate?' she suggested brightly.

The worried look that should not be a factory setting for a five-year-old reappeared. 'Cake is bad for your teeth.' The child raised her eyes from the plate of pastries on the table. 'I have very good teeth.'

'I can see that.'

A smile of pride appeared.

'You also have a lovely smile. Sorry about the cakes. I just thought for a treat...as it's a special occasion—our first morning—we might be naughty?'

The child's eyes grew round as she shook her head. 'I'm not naughty or I try not to be. Nanny Maeve says Papa was never naughty.'

Marco, who distinctly recalled his Irish nanny calling him a *limb of the devil* on more than one occasion, repressed a laugh, and closed the door behind him. The sound was drowned out by the new nanny, who showed less restraint in response to his daughter's claim. Her laugh was low and husky.

From where he stood, Marco got a good view of the puzzled expression on Freya's face but only the back of the redhead's burnished head as she turned the laugh into a cough.

'Does your papa have good teeth?' Kate asked, even though she already knew the answer to that one—his royal *perfectness* could have given an alpha wolf a run for his money.

Actually, now she thought about it, the wolf analogy was not such a terrible one, she decided, a little shiver slithering down her spine as she remembered his heavy-lidded steely grey eyes.

Shaking her head a little to dispel the image, she decided she had to be tolerant, which, despite her brother's accusations, she was. An only-child prince told he was perfect from birth—no wonder the man was so up himself!

She was nothing if not tolerant.

You could almost feel sorry for him, not that she did, but his daughter had clearly been raised to put her father on a pedestal and Kate knew well how that ended, when you inevitably realised the people you'd idolised had feet of clay. So, her sympathy was saved for the child's future disillusionment and her present isolated loneliness.

The former she couldn't do anything about, the latter she intended to. Her mind was buzzing with innovations to help this child discover fun.

'Papa never eats sweet things.' The little girl's voice halted. 'At least, I don't think he does. He doesn't like them.'

'Good for *Papa*,' Kate murmured under her breath, oblivious to the fact the words had reached the object of her sarcastic undertone.

Out of her line of sight the Prince moved into the room, as Kate dwelt contemptuously on the things that Papa, if the reports were to be believed, *did* like. Fast cars and tall, elegant, enigmatic, classy women, blondes, brunettes, redheads... Kate tucked behind her ear a strand of auburn hair that had escaped the fat ponytail that fell down her slender back, and diverted her thoughts before her imagination gave the redhead in a clinch with the Prince features or an extra six inches.

She could not imagine a scenario where the tag of *irresistible* attached to a man's name did not make her wince and it was used overtime when Marco Zanetti's name came up.

Still, she could forgive him for being far too good-looking if he'd just give a little of his apparently precious time to his daughter.

Kate felt an ache of sympathy for the child, anticipating the day when Freya realised that the figure she appeared to idolise was several light years away from perfect.

'Do *you* like sweet things? Cakes or sweets…chocolate…?' She ticked the treats off on her fingers.

'I don't know.'

It took Kate a few moments to realise that the child was speaking literally. Her professional scruples about respecting parental wishes slid away. 'Well, it's very important to look after your teeth.' She displayed her own, which were pearly white and even, barring a slight gap between her front ones. 'I like chocolate, but I wouldn't eat it for breakfast…unless, obviously, it was my birthday.'

The little girl stared at her with the expression of someone encountering a foreign life form.

'You eat chocolate for your breakfast?' She regarded Kate with a mixture of awe and horror.

'Well, birthdays are special and a little treat occasionally is nice.'

CHAPTER FOUR

Freya watched as Kate popped one of the pastries into her mouth whole.

'Mmm…that was lovely.' Kate sighed, smacking her lips and leaving buttery crumbs around her mouth.

The little girl gave a giggle. 'You have sugar on your nose!'

It was the smothered giggle that stopped Marco, who was about to reveal himself to the oblivious pair, in his tracks. He couldn't remember the last time he'd heard his daughter *giggle*. Her solemnity and her slightly accusing stare, or so it always seemed to him, had been something else that had reminded him of her mother.

One of the many *somethings* that had made him limit his contact with his daughter. Better by far to be a distant father than a terrible one, one not deserving or capable of returning her love. He had no idea if it was genetic, but he did remember the day that he had discovered his father was not a hero. He would spare Freya that disillusion.

Who are you protecting, Marco, asked the unsympathetic voice in his head, *her or yourself?*

Now able to see Kate Armstrong's face, he watched as, head tilted back, his daughter's new nanny went cross-eyed pretending to try and reach her nose with her tongue, while her charge fell off her chair onto the floor, laughing helplessly.

Kate wrinkled her nose. 'Have I got it?'

'No, let me...'

Kate turned her head literally as he spoke. A split second previously she had spotted him in the periphery of her vision. Shock nailed her to the spot as he planted himself beside her chair and leaned down.

It felt far too close and far too personal, close enough for her to feel the warmth of his body, and see the faint white scar on his lean cheek, white against the bronze.

Her nostrils flared and her stomach quivered in response to the clean male scent of him. He leaned in and touched the pad of one thumb to the sugar crumbs on the side of her nose.

The eye contact was infinitesimal but long

enough to send her pulse rate into the stratosphere and her stomach into a deep dive.

He didn't straighten up fast enough and the nerve-shredding interval necessitated several deep breaths before she could respond.

Oh, hell, what a time for her hormones to come out of hibernation!

'Thanks.' She didn't make the mistake of eye contact a second time. Instead she focused on the little girl who was trying to get his attention. It made her want to kick him for not noticing.

Even surfacing from her semi-catatonic state Kate recognised that the child wanted to fling herself at her father—had his arms opened even a little she'd have been in there, but they didn't and slowly Freya's little smile wobbled.

Kate's heart broke, her empathy swiftly followed by a rush of anger that freed her from the last lingering wisps of brain fog. *Oh, God, you stupid man!*

For a split second as his head turned and her eyes were once more captured by his cold hard gaze she really thought for a horror-struck moment that she had voiced her thoughts out loud.

'Hello there, Freya, are you being a good girl?'

Too good, Kate wanted to yell as she

watched the stilted exchange between father and daughter.

'Good morning, Ms Armstrong. I would ask you if you slept well but I suspect you didn't.'

Kate hoped he was rudely referring to the bags under her eyes and that he had no insight into the dreams she had fought her way out of every time she had dozed off, leaving her guilty and exhausted. A situation she blamed on the flight.

'I slept very well, thank you.' She lifted a hand to her left eye to still the contradictory flutter of her left eyelid.

Marco watched as she rose from the awkward position on the chair in one fluid graceful motion—any clumsiness on her part had obviously been feigned for comic effect.

The sinuous action grabbed him below the belt, reinforcing the artistic analogy that had occurred to him in the early hours when his brain would not switch off. She looked as if she had stepped right out of a Degas painting—a warm, breathing version of one of those slim supple ballerina figures, all graceful, slender, boneless limbs and big eyes.

There were a handful of people in his life who gave it to Marco straight and none of them were female—his mother thought the best of everyone—but even his critics had never displayed the open angry contempt that was sparkling in this woman's tawny eyes.

Kate was on her feet but had not gained any advantage, because the Prince still towered over her. She refused to acknowledge the physical or, for that matter, every other advantage in life this man had over her.

She wasn't impressed by an accident of birth or by the fact that fate had given him perfect everything and then an added extra wow factor ingredient...that was just luck. It would have been different if he were something she could admire—like a good, caring father.

Even if he hadn't been the breed of male who took it for granted that he ruined a woman's sleep—admittedly there were probably more than a few women who would have paid good money to have him disturb their sleep—his attitude to his daughter would have made her despise him.

She had already decided her strategy on the next official meeting was to be cool and totally professional. That was the best way to deal with men like this in her experience—not that men like this were in her experience.

Unfortunately the professional, cool message hadn't reached her eyes, which slid of their own volition to the moulded contours of the Prince's sinfully sexy mouth. The sculpted cruelty of the thinner upper lip contracting with the sensual fullness of the lower.

She moistened her own lips and congratulated herself on the fact he wouldn't be wasting his empty charm on her. She didn't feel lucky though, as his mobile mouth lifted in one corner and her stomach gave an elevator lurch. She felt fascinated.

Watching him could, if a person was not careful, become compulsive viewing. The way he moved made her think of some feral creature you recognised the beauty of but that beauty hid danger. Not to her though—that much had been made clear during a conversation at breakfast.

The conversation had turned to men after a handsome, bold-eyed young man, whose strut had made it clear he would have agreed with the description, had walked past and paused to smile at Kate.

'I dated him,' one of the other women at the table had told her. 'Good for fun,' she admitted to a chorus of giggles. 'But if you were looking for anything serious…?'

Kate said thanks for the tip, but she wasn't looking for anything serious or, for that matter, *fun*—not that sort anyway. Nobody believed her and supplied a list of men who might make her change her mind.

'Of course, Luisa has already got the best-looking guy in the place.' The woman in question looked smug and extended a finger with a sparkling ring on it for Kate to admire. 'Obviously he doesn't hold a candle to the Prince.'

'Oh, has anyone dated him?'

The comment turned all eyes on Kate.

'We should be so lucky. But the Prince is a gentleman. He doesn't mess with employees.'

'Understandable,' someone said behind their hand and others on the table exchanged significant looks.

Kate missed the significant looks. She had been too busy choking on her cereal after hearing Marco Zanetti, with his devilish grin, described as a gentleman.

'The…the storm last night didn't disturb you?'

Determined not to give him the satisfaction of reacting to the gleam of mockery Kate decided was shining in the Prince's eyes, she was still choosing her words carefully when her charge diverted his attention.

'She has ear things, Papa.' The child put her fingers in her ears.

'How do you know?'

'I had to shake her, just a little bit, to wake her up.'

Marco watched as Kate blew a strand of her hair from her face. She wrinkled her nose, frowning in concentration as she pinned the hair behind her ear. It was mundane but, watching her, he experienced a rush of excited anticipation in his veins unlike anything he had felt in a long time.

'Was I snoring?' Kate teased, shaking her head and creating a ripple in the waving heavy ropes of gleaming coils that lay down her narrow back.

She hadn't been asleep but the touch had made her leap a foot or so off the bed. She must have looked almost as shocked as the kid who had stood at the bedside looking at her with big terrified eyes as she introduced herself, in case, presumably, Kate had forgotten who she was, with a formal little curtsey in her cotton teddy-bear-printed pyjamas, insisting with shaky bravado when the room was illuminated by a flash of lightning that she was not scared of storms because storms were just science, and anyhow they had very good security.

Kate had replied that she was right, only Kate herself was a little bit scared so would Freya mind awfully keeping her company for a while?

Looking relieved, the little girl had crawled under the duvet at the bottom of the bed and into Kate's heart at the same time. She had fallen asleep about an hour later and had stayed sound asleep when Kate had scooped her up and tucked her back into her own bed when the sun appeared.

'Girls don't snore, it's science,' the little girl announced, her confidence slipping slightly as she looked to her father for reassurance. 'Do they, Papa?'

Kate turned her head and got a little shock as she encountered his enigmatic metallic stare. The insidious desire she was uneasily conscious of flared up hot. She wanted to look away, but she couldn't.

'Papa…?'

The spell broke and Kate shook her head, feeling stupid and also wary.

It took Marco a couple of seconds to focus on his daughter, for the thud of blood in his ears to grow quiet enough for him to respond.

'I've never heard a lady snore.' It was the literal truth. He had also never seen a woman without full make-up, which was why he had only just realised that the new nanny was not wearing any. His fingers flexed involuntarily as the thought of touching that skin embedded itself firmly in his head.

It was not his habit to spend the night with a woman. Love-making did not leave him feeling relaxed. He had never seen the appeal of pillow talk or the illusion of post-coital intimacy and during his marriage he and Belle had had separate rooms. He liked his own space and she had not questioned the arrangement, but then she wouldn't have, he thought bleakly.

'I do snore.' He returned his focus to Kate, who was biting her lip.

'Who told you that?'

Kate responded to the taunt with a thin smile. 'My brother always said he could hear me through the wall.' Though the walls in their three-bed semi were a lot thinner than the several feet of stone here, and neither of them lived at home any more.

'You have a brother?'

Even without the flinch, the way her face closed down, he could tell he'd hit a nerve. Even if he had made the effort to locate this nerve he wasn't sure he could have. This woman seemed to have almost as many shields as she did prickles.

He watched her notice he was staring at her hair—it was hard to miss it—and found himself saying, even though he didn't need to explain himself, 'Are you alike? I mean...' he nodded to her shiny head, imagining the silky threads running through his fingers like liquid fire '…red hair runs in families.'

'No, I…he…we…we were adopted.' They were words she had never said out loud before and the effort it had taken to push them out did not receive a corresponding momentous response, just a shrug and the impression he'd tune her out the moment he left the room.

She might have suspected he was making conversation just to be polite, except he didn't seem the type to feel the need, especially with a staff member, even if she was allowed to sit on the next-to-the-top table.

She was sure if she had accepted her place on her designated table she would have heard a much better class of gossip. As it was, she had gleaned some very interesting facts, like the guest list at the ball that was due to be held to celebrate the King and Queen's golden jubilee. A model whose name had been linked to the Prince had been invited, which was creating a lot of speculation.

Kate had looked suitably interested, even though it seemed to her that this didn't make the woman that special. The women the Prince dated might be a select club but the membership was not small.

She would have loved to be able to dismiss

him as a playboy prince, but the general consensus was that he worked as hard as he played and was considered to bring with him a wind of welcome changes. So, she was going to reserve judgment.

'I wish I had a brother,' the little girl said wistfully. 'But I need a mummy first.'

Kate turned her head but before her glance reached the child her eyes got enmeshed in the smoky silver stare of the father. The raw emotion written there only lasted a moment before his mask slid into place but the knowledge that the bleakness and pain existed came as a shock to Kate.

It had loosed something inside her that she didn't want to feel…she didn't want to name… Sympathy.

He held her gaze for a further uncomfortable moment, the laser-steel stare seeming to dare her to feel what she was feeling.

Which was fine by her. For once they were on the same page. *I don't want to feel anything around him*, she thought fiercely… Well, mild contempt, she could live with that.

It wouldn't be *mild* though, that was the problem. Nothing she felt about him was mild, it was extreme. And not just over the top, but liable to swing from one extreme to the other.

She didn't actually break free from the stare

until he released her. She took a deep breath to compensate for the fact she had been holding her breath and hid behind her thick straight eyelashes.

Marco had been waiting for the pity to die, and it did, but in its place... Analysing those last few moments, he decided that chemistry covered it, but whatever the name you used she was hiding from it. He controlled it ruthlessly, because it wasn't going anywhere. She was off limits.

'I'm sorry...' she muttered.

'For what?' His voice was hard as iron filings.

She lifted her head, feeling as awkward as hell. 'Your wife... I...sorry,' she ended feebly.

Can you ever just say nothing, Kate, or at least not the first stupid thing that pops into your head?

During breakfast she had barely been able to stop reacting with an eye roll when the table discussion had briefly drifted to the Crown Prince's tragically short marriage. 'Never a voice raised in anger,' someone had said to a murmur of agreement.

But that look she caught...the real pain... Her cynicism had taken a serious hit. Just because he was an arrogant pain didn't mean he hadn't loved and lost the woman he had intended to spend the rest of his life with.

Her glance was drawn to the wide gold band on his finger. Whoever came along to fulfil the advertised role of mother and lover would have quite an act to follow—it was hard to compete with a ghost.

Good luck to her, Kate thought, trying to conjure some sympathy for the future bride and failing—maybe it wasn't very sisterly but surely any woman who married this man would know exactly what she was getting.

'I just came to—'

'See Freya,' said Kate, who knew full well he had come to check up on her.

He responded to the smooth interruption after a short, startled silence with a tip of his head.

'Well, it's great timing. I was just going to order some outdoor play equipment. Freya and I are going to start on a collage this afternoon. Perhaps your papa would like to help you collect some things outside—leaves…twigs… And I wonder where Nanny keeps her glitter.'

'Glitter!' the little girl echoed, round-eyed.

'Don't worry, I'll find some,' Kate tossed over her shoulder with airy confidence.

Marco watched her go, a reluctant, admiring gleam in his eyes, well aware that he had just been ruthlessly manipulated. She had balls, he would give her that, but that did not mean he was going let it pass.

The other side of the door, Kate took a step into the sitting room and, backing into the wall, leaned weakly against it, the adrenaline rush making her knees shake, but before she could nurse the triumph the door opened with no warning.

Marco Zanetti stood in the open doorway saying loudly, 'I have an idea about the glitter.' Before he added, 'Be right back with you, Freya!'

'Glitter?'

Marco closed the door and got straight to the point. 'Save your child psychology for the five-year-olds. I think you're a little out of your depth with the grown-ups.'

Kate levered herself off the wall. She had never liked confrontations but she was not going to back down from this one. 'I don't know what you mean.'

'The playing-dumb thing will not work with me. I *mean*, I will not be played. Certainly not by a woman whose sole role is to provide a safe, stimulating and educational environment for Freya. You will not designate me little tasks. I am not a five-year-old. Nothing else outside the nursery concerns you,' he outlined with biting emphasis.

Her apprehension was swallowed by a wave of anger. 'Well, that's me in my place,' she snapped out sarcastically. As if she were ever likely to forget what her place was in an environment where you were judged on which table you sat on. 'You say that Freya is my only concern, and I agree. Quite frankly, I don't give a damn about you except in the way it influences your daughter...she is *aching* for you to notice her. She is hungry for your attention.'

It was the verbal equivalent of having the rug pulled out from under his feet. In his head Marco was stretched out on the floor with her small foot on his chest.

'I do notice her,' he pushed out dangerously quietly, but she seemed oblivious to the danger, the warning.

'It's not her fault her mother died. What would your wife think if she knew that—?'

The slow-burn fuse finally reached the blue touchpaper and all Marco's hard-fought-for control snapped. He took a step towards her, his fury only increasing when she took an involuntary step back, seemingly intimidated by his sheer physicality and the waves of emotion rolling off him.

'That I am a cruel, unnatural father?'

Kate shook her head, desperately trying to back-pedal.

'I know you have other calls on your time, but this time with Freya at this age—it is such a small window, and before you know it it's gone, and Freya is lonely.'

He met her appeal with cold silence and an expression that would have made a stone wall look warm and yielding.

'If you can't, then she at least needs more social contact with children her own age, she needs...'

What he could not give.

'She is so isolated. Are there no other children in the palace her age?'

'It is a bit late to go into professional mode,' Marco bit back, seeing her flinch and telling himself her white face meant nothing whatsoever to him. Why would it? 'You may disapprove of me but I'm the only parent Freya has ever had, her mother's not here.' The words slipped under, around and through every steel impenetrable barrier he had ever erected.

Kate froze, her eyes sliding from the visible pulse in his temple to his grey metallic *hurting* stare. 'S-sorry?'

'Her mother never even got a chance to hold her!'

'I'm sorry.'

'So you keep saying. You ask about children—there are cousins. My wife had three brothers.'

'So...' she began eagerly.

'I have little contact.'

He responded to her wide-eyed look of enquiry with an impatient explanation. 'My wife's parents, both members of two of the prominent families on the island who run the show, or would like to, are divorced. That happened fifteen years ago now and the families are still at one another's throats. There is only one person they hate more than each other.'

'They don't like you!' she exclaimed and then blushed under his ironic stare. 'Obviously I don't need to know why...'

'You have no idea how relieved that makes me feel,' he drawled with a sarcastic smile.

Kate's lips clamped tight. He really was the most arrogant son of a...king and queen. *And your boss to boot*, supplied the cautionary voice in her head.

'So you knew your wife—?'

'Before she was my wife. Yes, for many years she was my best friend.'

The information was delivered in a matter-of-fact manner that somehow made the statement all the more heartbreaking.

As he watched Kate's jewel bright eyes

fill, he wondered just how someone who em-
pathised to this extent survived in the real
world.

'Perhaps we could make this about *Freya*?'

Kate's chin lifted; she was insane to feel
sorry for this man. She should save her sympathy for the woman he did eventually marry
because he was obviously still in love with his
dead wife.

'Fine, let's do that. So perhaps you could put
your feelings to one side and approach your
in-laws, this being about Freya and not your
feelings.'

His nostrils flared as the insult hit home. 'It
is always about Freya,' he ground out. 'Protecting her is always my priority.'

'Good,' she said with a display of brisk false
bravado as she brought her lashes down in an
ineffective shield against the silver glitter of
outrage in his eyes. When angry he was really daunting. 'What ages are the cousins…
their names…?'

'I have not the faintest idea.' Her face pre-
sumably reflected her shocked horror, as a
sighing sound of exasperation escaped his lips.
'I will discover this information, but after B…
Freya's mother died, her grandfather blamed
Freya. He will *not* repeat those words. I have

made that clear to him.' The emphasis in his bleak eyes made her shiver.

'I'm sure he doesn't think that way now. No one could. People say things in grief that they don't mean.'

'You excuse him...?'

'No, of course not, I...' She bit her lip, aware she had blundered into territory where she didn't have a clue what was going on.

'Not black and white...not binary.' Her brother's voice was so loud in her head it sounded as though he were standing behind her.

'I'm sorry...'

'So you keep saying.'

'I tend to say things without...'

'Yes, this I have noticed. You have strong opinions. I will listen to what you have to say about Freya's welfare, but only if your comments are professional and evidence-based.'

And then he was gone. His reaction was more than she could have hoped for, given the absolute mess she had just made of that. *Professional.* He was right. A professional distance was something she never normally struggled with and yet with this father and daughter her objectivity had vanished.

Her emotions all over the place, she followed

him back into the nursery in time to see him press a kiss to his daughter's head.

'Sorry I have to go…' Marco suddenly felt so weary it didn't really matter what excuse he gave. The endless list of duties meant nothing to his daughter, who could not filter out the bull… He could feel the amber gaze upon him and kissed Freya again.

Damn the woman, even if her only sin was to point out the obvious. The obvious that no one else had ever had the guts to voice: that he was a poor, pathetic excuse for a father, just as he'd been a poor excuse for a husband.

Maybe it was Kate's courage that had pushed him to say the things he had, share the things he had. It was as good a reason as any other to explain what had made him tell her private details he had never revealed to anyone.

Breathing in the scent of his daughter's hair for a final second, aware of the hard knot of loneliness in his chest he rarely acknowledged, he lifted his eyes, his gaze drawn as if under the control of some invisible force to where the slim figure stood watching them. Kate looked shocked. Strangely, considering he was not a man inclined to trust, he knew at some deep unfathomable level that had nothing to do with proof or logic that the secret, that any secret, was safe with her.

'Be good for...' his eyes slid to the petite figure watching him with big golden eyes and the word *nanny* just wouldn't come '... Ms Armstrong.'

He tipped his head towards Kate and the next second he was gone, leaving trails of energy that seemed almost visible in his wake.

'Right, what shall we do now? Would you like to play?'

'Read. I always read after snack time. I'm a very good reader.'

A few minutes into the reading session Kate was assailed by a suspicion. She tested her theory and her suspicions were proved correct. The little girl with the seemingly advanced reading age couldn't read a word. She had simply memorised it all.

CHAPTER FIVE

KATE PRIORITISED THE changes she intended to make, always supposing she had the opportunity, and high on her list was the abolition of the strict adherence to a timetable, which was fine when it gave a sense of security but destructive when it became stifling and inflexible.

Testing the water, she had casually floated the idea of a slight diversion from routine, which had resulted in confusion among the staff and her charge. She knew she would require some tact, diplomacy and determination.

After yesterday she could not claim that tact and diplomacy were her strong points. Her strong point was that she possessed the determination that would see her through. There were some advantages to being consider *mule-stubborn.*

On her second evening she made her first move. Kate waited for the two nursery maids who were on duty to appear after Freya had gone to bed.

When they did, she suggested that they might leave the collage-making messiness spread out on the table.

They had looked longingly at the pile of fabric scraps, leaves and gluey mess on the table, but they had worriedly gone along with her request, so Kate considered it a win, considering they had almost fallen down in a heap when she had asked them to call her Kate. They were baby steps but she would get there!

Returning to her own flat, she was contemplating a walk to orientate herself to the grounds. So far, she had only seen the area set out as an outdoor play area for Freya. The only piece of equipment that gave any hint of play was a swing. Kate intended to change that.

Her exit was delayed by the unexpected arrival of a visitor. The tap on the door made her heart thump. It would be just like Marco Zanetti not to recognise her off-duty time, but it would be very unlike him to tap. He was definitely not a tapping man—more a bang-and-demand or just-ignore-the-door man.

So by the time she had opened the door she was not surprised to find, not a six-four challenging figure, instead the plumply pretty figure of Lady Rosa with her head of dark, wiry grey-streaked hair.

The woman who had been Kate's reception committee the previous night had an impressive-sounding job title, but then so did every other person in the place, but by this point they had all blurred into one, so she stuck to Lady Rosa.

The older woman didn't stay long. She had just dropped by to see if there was anything Kate needed, any problems...?

There were, of course, but the problem in question was one that Kate knew she needed to discuss with Freya's absentee father before anyone else. When, of course, he decided to put in another appearance.

The fact he hadn't did not improve her opinion of him. Her slight thawing hardened into solid ice. Could he really not know that he had a child who was hungry for his attention? It made her want to shake some sense into him, though the effort would be wasted—the man was built like... Stomach muscles quivering, she sharply veered away from Marco Zanetti's build.

His no-show was frustrating professionally. Personally she could have done without seeing him ever again! But she wasn't going to allow personal feelings to get in the way of her doing her job well.

Her suspicions had not gone away and she had done her research. She was ready to present the facts demanded when he did decide to honour them with his presence. The lack of surprise at his no-show spoke volumes: no one was shocked. Everyone was so *understanding*. He was a busy man. Well, the photos in an old online article she'd seen had shown that he wasn't too busy to escort beautiful women with interesting back stories!

She popped back into the nursery to tell the young women where they could find her if she was needed.

'I've got my phone on me.'

'It's fine,' one assured her cheerfully. 'Nanny always used to have…' She paused to straighten her apron and a wicked voice in Kate's head filled in the gap with inappropriate suggestions… *A gin and tonic… Afternoon sex.*

She choked off a laugh and turned it into a cough.

'She had a nap,' the girl supplied. 'Are you all right… Kate?'

'Fine,' Kate said cheerily. She didn't need a nap or, for that matter, afternoon sex. With anyone, she added to herself, as a possible playmate for the latter option bounded lithely into her head unbidden.

She attempted to walk off her anger and general frustration in not being able to discuss Freya with her father. Since the storm had passed over, the weather on the island had reclaimed its reputation as a temperate paradise on earth.

She had explored only a fraction of the grounds, which, once you got beyond the formal gardens around the palace itself, were divided into a series of separate rooms. They were designed in such a way that you would be surprised by a sudden breath-catching view out over the city to the sea beyond and you could walk from a bog garden complete with dribbling fountains, springs and moss-covered statuary into a wild flowers meadow and then a walled kitchen garden smelling of herbs and greenhouses full of produce used in the palace kitchens.

She walked out of this area, eating a ripe nectarine she had picked, feeling more settled because she had made a decision. If the arrogant prince wouldn't come to the nursery, she'd take it to him...or rather, she'd take herself to him.

She frowned at the tortuous grammar of the thought, her feet crunching on the gravel path of an intricately designed parterre she had passed through as she'd left the nursery playground, which meant there should be... She looked for the gap in the high hedge and realised as she did so that this was not the same piece of formal garden.

The hedge was lower and... She stopped. It was low enough to see a dark head above it.

She yelled out and hit the ground running.

Jogging along the grassy path between two rows of tall sentinel horse—the trees in full blossom made her think, between breathless huffs, of the one at the bottom of their drive where, as kids, she and Jake had fought over the best conkers. She pushed through the feeling of intense loss.

She had managed to keep the dark head in sight but she was already red-faced and breathless, her desperate *hey!* came out a wheezy croak.

She paused a moment, hands braced on her thighs as she fought to catch her breath. Jake would have seen the hilarity of this situation. He would never have let her live it down.

The wave of loss this time was even more painful. It made her forget the stitch in her side. She and Jake shared no blood link but they shared more important links, a lifetime of links, which was why his betrayal hurt so much.

Should she make the first move? Call him?

Before she could get sucked any deeper into the circuitous internal argument in her head, the dark head disappeared and she set off in pursuit again, heading for an archway in the wall, relief flooding her as the dark head came back into sight.

'Wait! Hold on!' she yelled out, breathless as she made it through the arch at a sprint.

The tall figure remained oblivious. He wasn't running but due to his superiority in leg length and the fact she was out of breath the gap wasn't getting any smaller, and she had the mother of all stitches in her side.

Then, just when she thought she might have to admit defeat or at least lie down, he paused and bent over as though he'd dropped something. She took her chance and yelled.

'Wait!'

His head lifted and he straightened up. She was too far away to see his face, which was a blur, but she could make out his bare arms, dark against the white of a tee shirt. Her gaze didn't get any lower than the black shorts. One minute there was only the thumping of her heart and the sound of birdsong, the next it was chaos, yells and waving guns all around her.

The sinister black-clad men had appeared from nowhere. It felt like dozens but, in reality, there were three. One relaying staccato information into a mouthpiece, while they all carried guns.

They were yelling at her in Italian. Actually, it could have been anything—her faculties had frozen in shock and icy, sense-numbing fear.

She said something back to proclaim her innocence and assure them that she was harmless. It was a waste of breath as they continued to bellow over her and indicated she should lie on the ground.

It was beyond disorientating and surreal to find yourself in the scene of an action movie, cast as one of the bad guys. A push in her back she didn't see coming sent her onto her knees. It was at that point that all the yelling stopped as though it had been switched off.

There was just one voice now. Deeper, clipped, anger vibrating in every commanding syllable.

Relief so intense that tears came to her eyes washed over Kate. Slowly she lifted her head from her chest, where it had sunk. She saw the men in black had melted away, though she could hear the buzz of radio voices in the distance, and the man she had been pursuing was standing there.

She had caught him.

What was she going to do with him?

Her imagination, assisted by her hormones, supplied a stream of suggestions. It was shock, she told herself by way of an excuse, and she tried to think cooler thoughts.

One day she'd laugh about this with friends around a dinner table, but that day was a long way off. Right now, she'd settle for not having him guess her thoughts. Getting up would be good too. She took a deep breath and pressed her hands into the ground to help lever herself to her feet, but nothing worked. Everything shook, confirming her previous diagnosis of shock.

As she waited, their eyes met and she saw the anger in his face slide into another expression. Something that made her internal tremors worse.

'I think… I think I might be sick…' she warned.

As her head went down the last thing in the world she would have anticipated was Marco lifting the heavy ropes of hair from her face. She could feel his fingers cool on the back of her neck. He didn't say a word.

'I'm not going to,' she said finally as the waves of nausea passed.

The hand on the nape of her neck vanished

and he stepped away, waiting silently as she sat back on her heels, her hands on her thighs visibly shaking.

'Please do not be nice to me or I will cry,' she begged between her chattering teeth, as if this weren't a humiliating enough position to be in.

'I have no intention of being nice to you,' he promised grimly, reliving the moment that he had seen the security guards move to contain her.

They had been doing their job and his fear had been they would do it too well. They had not deserved his reprimand or the curt dismissal. She, on the other hand... His jaw clenched, and the muscles quivered as he ground his teeth.

Left with nothing to do but wait to regain control of her body, she took in his outfit, what there was of it. As distraction went it was a good one. Her covetous glance moved up from his bare feet shoved in a pair of leather sliders up strong, lightly hair roughened brown calves and deeply muscled bronzed thighs. His wet black shorts were the mid-thigh, low-on-the-hip variety and a sleeveless white vest revealed his muscular shoulders and biceps.

He had the sort of body that you saw on men who leapt off a diving board and arched through the air, throwing impossible shapes before they hit the water without a ripple. Sleek, streamlined, powerful—there wasn't an ounce of excess flesh to hide the taut, perfectly formed muscle beneath oiled smooth skin.

Marco dragged a hand through his hair and some of the excess water that came away with it splashed icy droplets on Kate's face, breaking her free of the sexual thrall that had gripped her.

Lust, mindless attraction, chemistry, she listed them in her head in the hope that facing her monsters would make them vanish...aware that the exercise did smack of something horribly close to desperation.

'You can't wander around at will. Did you not see the signs saying private?' he ground out, the fury etched on his face emphasising each plane and hollow. 'This area—' his expansive gesture took in the lush green they stood in and caused a sequence of fluid contractions of muscle beneath the listening golden skin of his torso '—is,' he spelt out, gouging out each syllable for biting emphasis, 'off limits to—'

'No one told me. Those men—' She stopped and looked around, half expecting to see them lurking, but there was no sign of them. 'Those men could have...' Conscious of the whiney note in her voice, she bit her lip. What was she making excuses for anyhow? She'd done nothing wrong.

'Those *men* were doing their jobs.' Pausing as she continued to crouch there looking like some sort of bewildered supplicant, he held out his open-palmed hands in a gesture of impatience. When she didn't respond to encouragement he snapped out, 'Get up!'

'Do not order me around...' Her angry defiance vanished in the blink of an eye. She bit her lip harder this time and admitted, 'I don't think I can.'

It was the ruefully reluctant admission itself that hit him in a spot he didn't want to acknowledge. He knew that it had hurt her to have to admit she needed help. Taking a step towards her, he bent forward and held out a hand. 'Come on!'

Shifting her weight to one side, she reached for the hand but before her fingers had made contact his had curled around her wrist. He casually hauled her to her feet and immediately let go, but Kate had not got her land legs yet and she staggered, grabbing for anything to stop herself falling.

The anything was his vest.

Both hands clutching the white fabric, damp from his body, she fell against him, experiencing an immediate thousand-volt shock that stopped her breathing. It was only the large hand that moved to the small of her back that stopped her sliding back down to her knees.

It was sensory overload, the heat of his body, the hardness, the warm male scent of him… Her nostrils flared, her eyes closed, as she dug deep to break free of the mind-numbing tsunami as she leaned, weak-kneed, literally plastered to his front. The tremors that had been shaking her took on a different quality, no longer fuelled by shock but by the breath-catching, illicit excitement swirling through her veins like champagne bubbles.

She could hear him swearing above her head, feel his breath in her hair on the side of her face as the hand in the small of her back slid around her waist. The other curved around her jaw, turning her face up to him.

'You are not going to faint.'

She wanted to tell him she never fainted, but her throat felt too thick and scratchy.

He studied her face. The dilated pupils leaving only gold rims. 'Take some deep breaths… not *that* deep…'

Reacting to his *give-me-strength* tone, she rallied slightly and rebutted shakily, 'I do not need you to tell me how...' *How to stay standing?*

Fighting the mindless hunger clawing in his gut striving to get a firmer hold, Marco swore and stepped back. 'Fine, you do not need me.'

Arms folded, he watched as she wobbled before, with another curse of defeat, he grabbed for her, but she backed away like a drunken tightrope walker, strangely graceful.

He huffed out a sigh of defeat and reached for her. She wheeled backwards, muscle memory co-ordination keeping her upright, and instead of his hands landing on her shoulders they came to rest either side of her face.

A face minus make-up and its usual fiery halo, the purity of her features washed pale by shock making her look even younger. Even though he knew this was an illusion—he had made a point of checking her age and knew she was twenty-seven—it did serve as a timely reminder of the very real but invisible barrier they stood on opposite sides of.

The barrier wavered as her heavy eyelids lifted and she looked at him with eyes that were so *hungry* it took his breath away. The promise of passion sending a thudding stream of neat hormonal heat through his body.

Still, he rose above his baser instincts,

though fingernails were involved this time. 'Next time,' he promised, reliving the blood-freezing moment that he'd recognised the figure surrounded by the men, crack marksmen all, whose jobs it was to protect him and his family, 'I'll cut out the middleman and shoot you myself. Do not,' he added with grim warning, 'say *anything*. Not a word!'

She blinked, a belligerent glitter cutting through the shocked glaze in her eyes. She didn't respond well to ultimatums and that went double when the person issuing them was this man. She didn't care how many titles he had, she was not going to be silenced.

'I…they could have shot me; I could have died!'

'Do not dramatise!'

The response struck her as not only unfeeling but hypocritical. 'But you said…' She lost what little colour she had. 'Oh, God, I really could have died,' she repeated in a barely audible whisper. Less drama and more acknowledgment of her mortality as she saw the image in her head of her parents when there was the knock on the door to break the news…seeing all the things she had never done that she wanted to.

Kate, head full of missed opportunities and

regrets, felt her lips respond to some invisible tug and land on his mouth. All the things... said the voice in her head.

She had no more control over the impulse than she would have had over the self-protective reflex that would have had her jerking her hand from a hot surface, except in this instance she was moving towards the danger, the *heat*.

Her hands were in his damp vest to give her enough purchase to stretch up her body. 'Thank you for saving me—' Her lips brushed his.

Danger, yes, she could feel the danger in the pit of her belly, not repelling but attracting, and cool.

Her lashes lifted off her smooth, flushed cheeks and her eyes met his. He grabbed for her, hauling her into his body, all mindless need and no logic.

The rest of her words were lost in the kiss that started out hard and angry and changed to something else, something deep, slow, seductive. Some previously untapped place in her core that had nothing to do with logic and self-preservation took over and she melted into the warm, explorative, heart-stoppingly exciting intimacy of his tongue and mouth, his taste, his scent.

With a small mewling cry vibrating in the back of her throat, she strained upwards to deepen the pressure, tangling her fingers in the dark hair at the back of his head and pushing her breasts against his hard chest.

A moment later, or it might have been an hour, she was standing on her own feet separated from all that warmth and hardness with several inches of cool air between them feeling *bereft*, her nostrils still full of the musky male scent of him.

Then stupid.

Marco stood there, dragging air into his lungs as he pulled back from the heat that had surged through all the barriers that had never failed him before. All it had taken was the touch of her warm lips.

The loss of control was all the more serious, dangerous, because the woman who had instigated this meltdown was in his employ. She worked for him. He'd crossed a line and he didn't even bother rationalising it, instead he went into damage-control mode. It wouldn't happen again, he told himself, regaining by painful increments his habitual emotional distance. The few extra feet of physical distance seemed a sensible back-up plan.

When she spoke, he registered she sounded dazed, appalled even. 'Did I start that?'

Could her action have been construed as an invitation to what followed? She had no words to describe the kiss. She hadn't known a kiss could feel like that, that you could feel *want* and need in your bones, in your skin, in the soles of your feet.

'Yes, but I finished it, and it is…' his steely eyes sought and found hers '…finished,' he said, for his benefit as much as hers.

She felt the heat run up under her skin, leaving it washed with soft rose. Oh, yes, she was getting the message loud and clear. Did the man think that she was going to pin him down and… *Given half the chance, Kate, who wouldn't?*

'I was in shock,' she said, observing with growing resentment that he had recovered his cool with remarkable ease. The idea that anyone could be that *hot* one minute and then be so *clinical* the next—warning her off. It was mortifying.

'You kissed me back.'

He could hardly deny it. He said nothing.

'What are *you* even doing here?' *Other than the fact he lives here, Kate, this is all his, you're just the nanny.* 'At least I have clothes on!' The shrill addition put a dangerous glow in his eyes that made the pit of her stomach dissolve.

'I've been known to wear less when swimming.'

Kate immediately saw him wearing less.

'Relax, *cara mia*.'

Kate was too busy staring at her clasped hands and no doubt resenting the languid advice to register that he looked less than relaxed himself, the nerve beside his mouth throbbing extra time.

'Sexual attraction is not something that can be rationalised so stop trying.' He had, simply because there was no logical rationale that could explain away the fact, *wanted* the taste of her. From the first moment he had set eyes on her he had been ravenous for it.

Now he had tasted her and he could move on. Been there, done that.

He almost laughed aloud at this piece of pathetic self-delusion. As he was mocking himself her lashes lifted, revealing layers of emotion in her golden eyes. Something in her gaze made him feel stripped bare of his normal protective layer.

'I'm not—' Kate stopped, her chest growing

tight. Was he? The idea excited and frightened her in equal measure.

'It is, however,' Marco continued, more to remind himself of the fact that she was off limits, 'something that can be controlled, so stop worrying. I will save you from yourself.' He would also do something about the recent imbalance in his work-sex life, which had a way of messing with a healthy man's head and his control.

Control that showed a danger of slipping every time he thought about how she had tasted, how she had felt... No, he would *not* remember, because this would be a complication too far.

He was not his father. Thinking of his father was the sense cooling reminder he needed.

The implication that she would be the one making the move brought a flush of outraged anger to Kate's face and helped clear the remaining sensual fog of confusion in her head.

'I can assure you that you are safe from me, Your...' Oh, God, she came up against the same stubborn mental block that she seemed to have with his title and stopped.

'It is Highness, but you can call me Marco.'

'Well, Your *Highness*...' she said, adopting an attitude of mocking disdain and thinking,

You are just too *stupid, Kate, you kissed him, you* wanted *to kiss him, you lost the moral high ground at that moment.* 'Forget it,' she suggested to him magnanimously.

The *I have* stayed silent, but was very much there, hanging in the air between them.

'Heightened emotions…' She managed a pretty credible shrug. 'I nearly got shot.' It got her off the hook, technically at least.

'Shot…a slight exaggeration.'

Her lips compressed and she swore softly under her breath. '*What* did my predecessor call you?' Not caring if the change of subject was not really subtle, she didn't want this conversation to move to a place that blurred any lines she had drawn in the sand.

His lips quivered slightly. 'Nanny Maeve knew me when I was seven.' *I never kissed Nanny Maeve*, he added silently.

Once was enough, he thought, looking at her mouth and thinking once was too much, a taste had made him hungry for more. As recreational drugs went, this woman's mouth had addiction written all over it.

'Well, I hope you'll be able to afford me the same professional courtesy you did her. I didn't intend to intrude but I spotted you and, as I was hoping to speak to you about Freya, I just—'

'Chased me.'

'Sorry if I interrupted your...swim...?' Not that she could see any sign of a pool.

'I was retracing my steps looking for my phone.' The recollection brought a frown to his brow.

Losing his phone made him seem almost normal but he wasn't, he really wasn't, he lived in a different world from the one she inhabited.

'I had assumed,' she continued frigidly, 'that I'd be able to make contact when you came to see Freya.'

He scanned her face with narrowed eyes. 'Do I detect a note of disapproval in your voice?'

'It's not my place to disapprove, as I'm sure you'd be the first to tell me, but I'm not sure how this works. Do I make an appointment?' She allowed her chilled question to hang there a moment before adding with barely disguised sarcasm, 'Or do I need to relay the information through some intermediary?'

If she had been hoping to elicit some guilty response, she failed, but the permanent groove between his brows deepened. 'Firstly, what you do *not* do is create a security incident, and if you have any information concerning my daughter there are no intermediaries, you contact me directly.'

'I was trying to.'

'Well, go ahead.'

Her eyes slid up and down his tall, angry, half-dressed frame. 'Here?'

'Why not?'

'I would prefer a more formal setting,' she announced stuffily, thinking, *With no ripped body clouding my judgment.*

He looked inclined to argue the point but shrugged. 'Fair enough. I can give you half an hour in my office. Is that *formal* enough for you?'

She ignored the mockery and nodded, following him across the green expanse of grass to the stone wall of a tower.

'It's a short cut.' He nodded towards a flight of steps cut into the stone. He paused at the foot and turned to her. 'You going to be all right with the steps?'

Her lips tightened. 'So long as there are no gun-toting ninja warriors hiding around the next bend, I'll be fine...'

'Right, then, after you.'

She stepped out smartly, not slowing even when her thigh muscles began to complain and burn. That was about the same time that she realised this arrangement gave him a very good view of her bottom. He was probably comparing it unfavourably with the innumerable curvaceous bottoms he knew intimately.

She glanced suspiciously over her shoulder and he smiled back innocently.

'You'd be insulted if I wasn't.'

Turning back, she stomped her way up the rest of the steps at a breakneck speed that reduced her legs to jelly by the time she reached the top, where she promptly forgot her aching legs.

'Oh, my goodness, this is...' She looked around, too enchanted to maintain her icy distance as she smiled. The swimming pool they were standing beside was built into the section of roof and surrounded by a terrace filled with lush greenery. It was stunning in itself, but it was the most spectacular view across the capital and out to sea that was truly breathtaking.

'This is your office?' she asked, thinking, *Nice work if you can get it.*

His lips twitched. 'No, but it does have access to my office. This way.' He opened a door that was partially concealed behind a classical statue of a bare-chested woman being ravished by someone Marco was probably distantly related to.

This time she followed him down the internal staircase and proved her moral superiority by not looking at his bottom, or not much.

'Take a seat.'

She looked around. There were options aside from the modern-looking chair behind the massive desk that was empty bar from a few monitor screens, an Anglepoise lamp and a photo, of what or who she couldn't see from where she was standing, but if the gallery of snaps on the wall of exposed stone were any indication they were of Freya. Or maybe his late wife. There were none of her on the wall, which seemed... *None of your business, Kate.*

The other two walls were covered floor to ceiling in bookshelves where the books were *not* colour coordinated, and a surreptitious glance at the spines suggested the collection was eclectic. The last wall was taken up by open leaded windows set in a deep stone embrasure that offered a view almost as good as the one from the pool.

She stood there for a moment feeling awkward before she selected one of the leather chesterfields and sat down.

'I'm just going to change into something less comfortable.' He flashed her one of his enigmatic smiles and vanished.

If he'd returned thirty seconds earlier, he would have found Kate studying the gallery of framed photos that covered one wall, trying to work out why a man who had this amount of photos was so physically absent from his daughter's life, but when he did emerge she had retaken her seat and was sitting with her hands primly folded in her lap.

His quick change had obviously included a shower. She could smell soap and shampoo mingled with his clean, inimitable personal scent as he walked past her to the desk.

His hair, wet and slicked back, curling on his neck, caught the light shining in from the window as he propped his denim-clad rear on the desk top and stretched his long legs out in front of him. His attitude was a match for the navy shirt, the sleeves of which he'd rolled up to reveal his sinewed bronzed forearms. He wore a pair of faded jeans that clung to his thighs in a way that made her tummy muscles quiver. All the laid-back designer casual contrasted starkly with the steely gaze he pinned her with—no casual there.

The moment stretched beyond what was polite, but then he clearly didn't think the normal social rules applied to him. He made his own rules.

'You look guilty. What have you been up to...?' Then, ignoring his own question, he spread his hands, palms up. 'So, what was so important?'

CHAPTER SIX

KATE TOOK A deep breath and tried to organise her thoughts into some sort of coherence.

One long finger had started tapping the polished surface of his desk. 'You have my attention.'

Which was part of the problem. His unblinking regard was unsettling. It was those eyes; she shook away the crazy idea that he could read her mind and cleared her throat, wondering if he had a timer going and any minute he'd look at his watch and say, *That's it for today.*

Or was that a therapist?

'It's about Freya.'

He did the brow thing again, his growing impatience communicating itself across the intervening space.

'Did my…?' Hesitating, she lifted her eyes from her contemplation of her interwoven fingers. 'Did the previous nanny ever mention Freya's reading?'

'She did say that it is very advanced for her age.'

'Ah…right. Well, her language is certainly extremely advanced for her age, and I can see how it might have looked to someone that her reading was too,' she said tactfully.

'*Looked* that way?' He shook his head and rose to his feet, towering over her, his eyes watchful and not friendly.

She'd seen defensive parents before but not as beautiful as him, none that made her tummy muscles quiver. None that had kissed her.

It was hard, looking at the compressed line of his lips and knowing that only minutes ago they had moved skilfully, sensuously, over her own, to think that this was the same man.

She tuned out the memory and painted on a professional smile, a bit frayed at the edges but it gave her the confidence to push on. 'Freya was eager to show off her skills. She is very eager to please.'

'Now why do I think you don't think that's a good thing?' he drawled.

Kate ignored his dry insertion. She couldn't afford to drift from the point. 'She appeared very fluent with her reading. In fact, streets ahead of the curve for her age.'

'Then what is the problem?' he asked, wondering if she was inventing some issue to make herself look important. He discarded the idea almost immediately. He had experience of women who would do any number of things to gain his attention but Kate Armstrong had not come across like that at all.

'The thing is she can't read, which would not make her unusual for a five-year-old, but there are some indications that there might be a problem.' It was blunt but sometimes blunt was the best way.

'That is ridiculous you just said yourself—'

'She isn't *reading*. She has memorised the texts of her favourite books. She has an extremely good memory, really very good, but that is often the way with people with dyslexia.'

'*Dyslexia!* You are saying my daughter is dyslexic, and you have picked this up within hours and Nanny Maeve didn't and she's been with Freya all her life.' His lips curled in expressive contempt as he hooked his thumbs into the belt loops of his jeans, his body language challenging her.

She nodded and stayed calm. The 'shoot the messenger' thing was not exactly unexpected.

'I know how it must seem but sometimes a fresh pair of eyes...' She swallowed a sigh, unable to detect any thaw in his hostile manner.

This was not going to be easy. 'This is no re-flection on...anybody... People with dyslexia are very good at disguising the fact,' she told him with diplomatic restraint. Privately she thought her predecessor had a lot to answer for. 'It's easy to miss.'

'Or invent,' he threw out. 'Some people will do anything to hog the limelight.'

In response to the insult, he received a com-passionate little smile that was all teeth-clench-ing understanding. He had never encountered a woman who grated on him more. Kiss her, throttle her—his reactions to her breathing were way beyond what was reasonable.

'I know this is a shock, but—'

Marco dragged a hand through his sleek wet hair, his jaw clenched and quivering. He found himself unable to keep the doubt from edging into his voice. 'I *would* have noticed...'

Sure, Marco, because you hear your daugh-ter read such a lot. The recognition added a fresh slug of toxic guilt to the burden he al-ready carried.

For a second Kate's compassion warred with her disapproval of his parenting style. Compas-sion won. It was not the first time she'd seen parents angry and in denial when they were told there was an issue with their child. This situation felt a lot... This was not like any job she had experienced. It wasn't as if ordinarily she forgot about work the moment she went home, there was always preparation, but she was able to switch off. Here, she felt immersed, and she was fast losing her professional distance, which, along with compassion, was in her view essential for a good teacher, or one that wanted to stay sane, at least.

'Look, I don't expect you to take my word for it,' she said, keeping her voice calm and unemotional. 'And I'm not suggesting for one moment that I'm an expert, but there are tests that would confirm the issue and I strongly advise that Freya have them. The earlier these things are picked up, the better.'

She hesitated a moment, worried she was throwing out too much information, before continuing. When people were shocked there was a saturation limit of how much they could retain.

'I have looked it up and your psychology department here at the university have just completed a world-class study.'

He looked down at her in silence, then, twisting away, walked around the desk before lowering his long lean frame into the leather chair behind it.

'How did we…how did I not pick it up?'

Kate didn't say anything. She suspected he already knew.

She watched, her heart squeezing in her chest as he picked up the photo from his desk and stared at it. Only a parent who loved their child could feel that sort of pain she saw written on his face: pain and guilt.

He put the photo down and, resting his elbows on the desk, looked up. 'Is there a cure?'

He already knew the answer. He remembered the boy at school who had been singled out by teachers and pupils alike as lazy and stupid. The fact that boy was now a man whose entrepreneurial skill had made his name world-famous did not alter the fact his schooldays must have been hell.

He would not let that happen to Freya.

'Is home schooling an option?'

It was, but not a good one as far as Kate was concerned. 'I think you're jumping ahead of yourself, and it's really not useful to think in terms of a cure. Freya is not ill. People with dyslexia, their brains are just wired differently but the earlier a diagnosis is made, the easier it is to formulate strategies which make life easier. But first I think you should get it confirmed…'

His curling lashes lifted off his razor-sharp cheekbones. 'You were sure enough to come here and…' His voice trailed away. He could have done without the insight that told him he was looking for someone to blame but himself.

Kate was really missing her professional distance. Her heart ached painfully with sympathy. If she had thought he was an uncaring parent, she was ready to admit she had jumped to conclusions.

'I told the truth.'

'As *you* see it.'

She nodded. 'I know you didn't want to hear this and I…' She lowered her gaze, not willing to acknowledge the level of her empathy for him, an empathy that went way beyond what she would normally feel. 'It's always best to tell the truth.'

The frown still stamped on his face, curiosity filtered into his silver eyes as he looked at her. '*Always?* Do you *really* believe that?'

Her delicate jaw quivered at the incredulity in his voice. 'Of course.'

'No exceptions?'

'No.'

'You have no doubts, do you? I almost envy your ability to see everything in black and white.'

His comment came so close to one of Jake's accusations that she flinched. A moment later she lifted her chin. 'Actions are right or wrong, they are either a lie or the truth.' She got to her feet. 'Finding out your life is a lie, that you are not—' She broke off, dodging his eyes.

It would be too much to hope that he'd miss the open goal she had just presented to him.

He didn't.

'Who lied to you?' he asked, probably imagining a cheating lover.

The sly question made her stiffen defensively. Even if it was a slightly off-target shot in the dark, it showed he possessed a spooky perspicacity, which made her deeply uneasy. She really did not want this man wandering around in her head.

Either he was way too sharp or those eyes really were X-ray and not just X-rated.

'I think we have rather drifted from the point.'

Which was that he was one hell of a father! Guilt curdled sourly in the pit of his stomach as he considered his arresting style. He'd farmed out his daughter to an elderly woman and then blamed her successor rather than place the blame where it lay, on his own shoulders.

'I actually find it kind of reassuring that little Miss Goody Two-Shoes is as messed up as the rest of us,' he drawled.

She compressed her lips over a retort. It took all her willpower not to respond, and focus instead on the cool professional advice she was meant to be delivering.

'Look, I know I've given you a lot to think about and it's hard to take in.'

She had no idea.

'I've made a list of articles, books that you might find helpful, but, as I say, I'm not an expert. Fortunately you have access to as many experts as you need.'

Freya would not be at the back of any queue, sad that she had the best of everything but all she wanted was her dad.

'I'll send you my personal email. Could we keep this between ourselves for the next few days?'

'As you wish,' Kate responded stiltedly. She had no idea why she felt so disappointed by this response. 'Dyslexia is nothing to be ashamed of,' she added, struggling not to show her contempt and, if his expression was any indicator, failing pretty miserably.

The heel of one hand pressed to his forehead, he looked at her for a moment and then appeared to come to a decision. 'I am not ashamed, not of Freya at any rate.' Her lips, compressed in a disapproving line, parted. 'I am going to share some information with you.'

Not obviously, because he cared one way or the other what her opinion of him was. It was simply that he didn't want her saying something that would come to the ears of the council.

'Do I have to sign the Official Secrets Act?' she asked, her flippancy masking her confusion, which turned to disquiet when he didn't smile.

'That will not be necessary.'

'I wasn't being serious.'

'At the ball next week I intend—' He paused and angled a questioning glance at her face. 'You have heard about the—?'

'Yes.'

He nodded and sketched a smile without humour. 'It is hard to keep a secret in this place.'

'The ball is a secret?'

'The announcement I am to make at it is.'

'You're getting married and you think your fiancée might have a problem with Freya's—?' Her hand went to her mouth. Had she really just said that out loud?

His deep bellow of laughter cut her off before she could dig herself a bigger hole.

'That is quite an imagination you have

there!' he said. His mild scorn made it worse
somehow, making her face burn. It would have
burned hotter had she known he was wondering if that fertile imagination extended to the
bedroom.

Marco took a deep breath. He wanted to have
sex with her, and he couldn't have it. It was
not a complicated concept to grasp and yet
his brain was still swerving around it, creating imaginary steamy scenes that were never
going to happen.

'I am not getting married, and when I do
it is Freya who will be the one giving *her* approval, not the other way around. When she's
older she'll need a female role model...'

Kate noted the revealing fact that love didn't
feature at all and felt a stab of sympathy. 'Poor
woman!' she exclaimed without thinking.

His dark brows shot up as he slumped with
elegant negligence into his chair, spinning it
back a couple of feet across the wooden floor
to see her better. She knew the pose of lazy
grace touched by decadence was an illusion.
No man had a body like his without some
pretty stern self-discipline.

'You think being my wife, the future Queen,
makes someone an object of pity?' He posed

the question, anticipating her discomfort. 'I wish you'd tell that to the women queuing around the block to interview for the vacancy.'

Kate's jaw literally dropped at this addition—outrageous even for him. The knot of incredulity in her chest bubbled to the surface and she laughed.

'You have my sympathy. It must be *so hard* being catnip to the opposite sex.'

When they were handing out ego he really had stood in the line several times, but then if you looked at that face in the mirror every day who wouldn't be arrogant? Her glance drifted to his sensual mouth. Where kissing was concerned he had the right to be arrogant, and if his skill at love-making was even a fraction as skilled... Unable to cling to her mockery and painfully aware of the ache between her legs, she found herself staring helplessly at the fascinating symmetry of his face. It was a face that in all its moods exerted a troubling fascination for Kate, a fascination that exposure didn't diminish, but fed.

Head dug deep into the leather head rest and tilted to one side, in a what she was recognising as a characteristic gesture, he made some elegant adjustments to his posture and swirled the chair from side to side.

He laughed, the deep sound warm and uninhibited. Kate felt the rumble under her skin as a tingling warmth.

Helpless not to, she found herself smiling back.

God, what could he do if he put some effort into being charming?

She dodged the worrying answer to that one.

'Oh, I'm under no illusions. I know it's the crown that is the attraction. I will not expect any future bride to pretend otherwise.'

'Oh, I don't know about that.' The unwise words were out there before she could stop them.

He tipped his head in acknowledgment and she blushed. His smile faded into a sombre, introspective look.

'I would not expect a future bride to pretend to be in love.'

'But what if she is?'

'Then I would not be marrying her.'

Because he thought he'd never love anyone the way he loved his first wife?

'I think that is sad.' She felt her cheeks flare again as she gnawed on her full lower lip. 'I spoke out of turn.'

'It's not stopped you so far,' he inserted drily as he pulled himself upright in one smooth, graceful motion. 'So please enlighten me as to what is *sad.*' He managed to keep his voice totally neutral, but still imbue his words with cheek-stinging sarcasm. It was a neat trick that had probably taken years of practice.

She took a deep breath. It was hard to be sympathetic to someone who gave a new meaning to unpleasant.

'Freya's mother, it was tragic, but some people do fall in love again, you know.'

Her interpretation of his comment stopped him dead in his tracks. He wondered how fast that idealistic glow of compassion would fade from her eyes if she knew the truth—that he'd killed Freya's mother.

The doctors could talk about her ruptured uterus and massive blood loss, but he knew differently.

'Is that your experience?' he countered softly, and watched her eyes flare in alarm before the barriers were raised.

'Oh, I've never—' she began, stopping as she heard the echo of her brother's accusations in her head.

Jake would have said no man ever reached her high standards, but it wasn't that at all. She was what some people might call a closet romantic. She really believed in soulmates, that there was someone who completed you out there.

She didn't think everyone was lucky enough to find theirs, but she didn't want to settle, which didn't mean she hadn't dipped her toe in the dating waters, it was just that she'd never really gone any farther, which had led her to the conclusion that she really wasn't that highly sexed.

A conclusion that had just been thrown into doubt by a kiss. Not just the kiss, the fact she had not wanted it to stop. The inconvenient possibility that the wrong...*very* wrong man, and not the man who was her perfect match, would awaken her dormant sexuality had never even crossed her mind.

She had always felt confident about her choices, but her right-and-wrong, black-and-white world view was taking some serious hits and the problem was that once you started questioning *one* certainty you started questioning everything!

'I have been very busy with my work, career.' Able to hear the defensive note in her voice, she brought her lashes down in a protective sweep.

'Climbing the greasy ladder,' he drawled, recognising the lie but letting it go. 'And then you leapt off,' he added, miming a diving gesture with his long fingers. 'Curious?'

She compressed her lips and clung to her defiance. 'I have always wanted to travel.'

'You really are a very bad liar, but shall we get back to my announcement? As things stand at the moment, when I die Freya is first in line to the throne, but should she have a male sibling he would take precedence.'

This man was so vitally alive, the most alive person she had ever met, to think of him not *being* around set off a discordant note of denial in her head.

'Freya does talk a lot about a brother.'

'You're telling me I should hurry up? I think I have a few years left in me yet.'

His mercurial mood shifts made Kate feel constantly on edge, and his lazy mockery made her teeth clench. Ego was not an attractive thing even when justified, and his was. His sexual potency entered a room before he did!

'The point is,' Marco continued, picking up his original thread, 'as things stand a younger brother would be heir.'

'Primogeniture.'

'Exactly, well, I have dragged the royal council kicking and screaming to the point where they are willing to sign off on the change. If they learned that Freya has anything *they* consider a handicap...' he emphasised, forestalling her protest, 'keeping in mind,' he added drily, 'that most of them have not changed their minds about anything since birth...they are so risk averse that some might consider that something as simple as red hair...' his eyes came to rest on a rope of curls that lay against her neck 'might set a dangerous precedent. You get my drift?' he said, thinking of those ropes of russet gold against his skin as she sat above him.

She nodded. 'Does Freya know?'

'Not yet.' Marco was unwilling to acknowledge he had not thought that far ahead. Had he worked so hard to gift his daughter something that he hadn't considered her rejecting the gift? Maybe she wouldn't want equality if equality meant her future was mapped out as his was.

'Will she be at the ball when you do the big reveal?'

'Freya!' he exclaimed. 'I don't think that would be—'

'Oh, she'd love it,' Kate cut in, seeing the smile on her charge's face if she could walk out beside her father. 'She'd be so proud to walk in there with you. She should just put in an appearance, of course,' she added hastily. 'It's not

like she'd be there until the small hours…?'
Head tilted to one side, she looked at him ap-
pealingly.

'Am I being manipulated, Kate?'

She shook her head, genuinely confused by
the accusation. 'Of course not. I just thought,
if she hates the idea she can sit somewhere and
watch with me.'

'Sit and watch…' he said slowly. 'A delight-
ful, if slightly Victorian image. I shall invite
my daughter to the ball, but you will of course
need to accompany her and whisk her away
like a mini-Cinderella before the guests start
misbehaving.' *If only*, he thought. The formal
occasions were suffocating not scandalous.

Kate could not hide her horror at the pros-
pect. 'But I couldn't. I don't…'

'Consult with my mother on clothes, accessories and such—despite appearances she has
a very good sense of fashion.'

'The Queen? I couldn't possibly…maybe
Lady Rosa. She seemed…'

'Charming? Oh, she is,' he said with an edge
to his voice. 'But do *not* go to Lady Rosa.'

Despite the dismissal, Kate felt inclined to
argue the prohibition. As mental images of the
woman flashed into her head, she conceded
that the woman was possibly not very stylish,
certainly not as elegant as the pictures she'd

seen of the Queen. Still, Lady Rosa was less regal but much more approachable than the actual monarch.

Kate was already dismissed, his fingers moving across one of the keyboards on his desk. 'And do not use her as an intermediary to my mother,' he added without looking up.

She shook her head in bewilderment even though he couldn't see her. 'But why not?'

He looked up then. 'Because, Kate, Lady Rosa is my father's mistress and there is a limit to *civilised*.' At least for him there was.

CHAPTER SEVEN

'Oh, yes, that one is perfect… Oh, but the bra will definitely have to go.' The Queen turned to her granddaughter, who was dancing around in a pink ballerina dress. 'Don't you think so, Freya?'

The child paused to consider the subject, her expression so like her grandmother's that for a moment Kate forgot she was stressed as hell by the whole process and laughed.

'I think you're right, Grandma…no bra. Oh, I think I'm beautiful,' she added, swirling in front of the mirrors that covered one entire wall.

'Oh, you are!' both women exclaimed in unison and exchanged a smiling glance.

The Queen, despite her patrician looks, was possibly the least regal person Kate had ever met. She exuded a warmth, professed herself to be *quite lazy* and didn't appear to be tuned into the palace gossip machine at all. She was definitely not Kate's image of a wronged wife. She didn't seem angry, bitter or downtrodden. She seemed a woman who was very comfortable in her own skin.

But behind the *lazy* facade she could be relentless when she made up her mind, which was why Kate was standing there in the most fantastic dress she had ever worn being told her bra would have to go.

She was not going to accept the dress. She was just humouring her royal companion.

'I really don't think... It's beautiful but I don't *need* a dress and I couldn't possibly afford...' Her voice trailed off as she glanced at her reflection in the wall of mirrors in the body-hugging, deceptively simple bias-cut slip of blue silk, and she sighed, admitting, 'It is lovely.'

'It is perfect, and the matter is settled. As for the cost, Marco is picking up the bill. This is a work-related expense.'

Kate's husky laugh rang out. 'He'll be furious,' she added, sobering.

'This is his instruction, my dear,' the Queen inserted gently.

Kate looked doubtful. He might have said dress, but he could not have meant a dress like this.

'Now,' the Queen added briskly. 'Shoes. You

have tiny feet,' she observed, looking at the trainer-clad feet exposed as Kate lifted the hem of blue silk.

Half an hour later, the items wrapped in layers of tissue were packaged up and stacked, waiting to be carried to the waiting car.

'We must do this more often,' the older woman said, turning to Kate with her warm smile. 'I can't remember the last time I had such fun.'

Kate, who could not imagine another occasion when her role would involve picking out a designer evening dress and accessories, gave a non-committal cover-all grunt and smiled. She had, despite all her misgivings, enjoyed the day.

Outside on the wide tree-lined street, which housed a row of high-end designer shops to rival any capital city, the air was warm but not unpleasantly so. Kate inhaled the smell of the horse-chestnut blossoms and sneezed violently.

The allergy coming back to haunt her.

'Are you all right?'

'Fine,' Kate assured the older woman. It seemed incomprehensible to her that the King should humiliate her the way he did by keeping a mistress that it transpired everyone knew about.

'Freya is happy. I think that is down to you, so thank you.'

'Not at all, it is my—'

'Ah, duty… I know about duty, my dear.' She touched Kate's face, her expression wistful, or was Kate just imagining that because she felt sympathy for the woman's position? She wasn't sure. 'I admit I cannot get excited about babies, but Freya is just becoming *interesting*, don't you think? Marco, of course, was always interesting but so very…self-sufficient, even as a child.'

Kate, who didn't have a clue how to respond to the information, just nodded.

'Now we will take afternoon tea, unless you share Nanny Maeve's disapproval of such indulgences…?'

'I don't.'

'It's fine,' piped up Freya. 'Kate has lovely teeth and it's a celebration, we can have chocolate.'

'Well, that is settled, then,' her grandmother said, looking amused.

It was just left to Kate to follow meekly behind. The parcels were piled into a waiting car and the Queen announced they were going to walk to the tea shop.

The information that they were walking had created a flurry of activity as the security detail adapted, clearly not thrown by the Queen's mercurial change of timetable.

The Queen watched with a benevolent smile as her security team swung into action. 'This… they are Marco's doing. I used to cycle around the city with no issues, but he is so overprotective, especially where Freya is concerned.' Her glance went to the little girl, who was skipping along happily. 'Understandable, but he means well. I was so happy, we all were, when he had someone to share his life with, and Belle always adored him. Such a tragedy and he never talks about it. But that is Marco's way, strong and silent. Here we are.'

One of the security guards emerged from the café, his nod presumably conformation that it was safe for them to enter.

There was a perimeter of empty tables around the table they were led to.

'I want a chocolate milkshake.'

'It is always good to know what you want and go for it,' the Queen said, requesting iced tea for herself. When asked Kate said iced tea would be nice.

'Freya is the image of her mother. Belle was always a pretty child. It was such a wicked loss.' She sighed. 'For a long time after her death I feared for Marco. He shut himself off and...' She shook her head. 'He was in a dark place.'

'I can't begin to imagine what it would feel like,' Kate reflected, watching Freya, who was slurping a milkshake noisily through a straw. 'To make a new life with someone you love and then at the perfect moment everything falls apart...'

Did you ever recover from something like that? Or did you just go through the motions... functioning compared to living?

Recalling his comments about his future wife, she didn't think that Marco had; his scars might be the invisible variety but the past was still impacting his life.

'Everyone was distraught. Belle's family—' The Queen cleared her throat. 'It was understandable, I suppose, people in pain hit out.'

'Yes, Marco... Prince Marco,' Kate corrected with a self-conscious blush, 'did mention what happened.'

The Queen's feathery brows lifted in surprise. *'Did he?'* she said, an alert look sliding into her eyes. 'My son is not known for sharing...and a *lot* falls on his shoulders. It has done from an early age. His marriage may have ended but I think that Marco is married to this land, this country... It makes me sad that he has no one to share the burden with now.'

Before Kate could think of how to respond to this flow of confidences, the Queen rose to her feet displaying an energy a woman half her age would envy as she announced it was time to leave.

As the security detail rose from the tables they occupied she pitched her voice loudly. 'Actually, the cycling is good for these men. I have actually improved their stamina.'

Kate laughed, more confused than ever that a man who had a wife like this would choose to keep a mistress who, by any conventional standard, was far less attractive. And how did the Queen cope with the humiliation of everyone knowing about his mistress? The arrangement seemed crazier than ever to Kate.

She thought her own family was odd, but by comparison...

His mother had reported in her own inimitable way that she liked the new nanny. 'So easy to talk to...don't you think so, Marco?'

It was a given his mother would love Kate. His mother would have seen the good side in a serial killer, it was just the way she was, but her insistence was particularly vehement when she spoke of the English nanny.

'Do not hurt her though, Marco. I think she is very empathic. It makes her vulnerable.'

Marco had no intention of hurting her, and he was here to see his daughter, not her disapproving nanny, who, when he'd entered, had been standing in the middle of the room, dancing with his daughter in something that was vaguely recognisable as a waltz.

'Papa, I have a beautiful dress and I had chocolate milkshake with cream on top. I had a moustache! And I am learning to dance, see?' Freya gave a wobbly twirl to illustrate the fact.

Watching, Kate found there was something endearing about the awkward way he ruffled the child's hair. The fact he was making the effort made her throat ache with emotion.

'It sounds like I missed a lot of fun,' Marco observed, his eyes sliding to Kate, who had not moved since he'd entered. 'Are you going to show me your dress, Freya?'

'You want to see my dress?'

Her astonishment sent a slug of guilt through Marco, who found himself remembering the way he had sought his own father's approval, how much an 'Excellent' or a pat on the head had meant to him.

'Yes, I would.'

Freya's eyes went to Kate, who nodded, and the child rushed off.

Kate walked over to her phone and switched off the music that had been playing in the background.

'So you are a dance teacher too?'

She shrugged. 'I took lessons for a while.'

'Are you good?'

'Not good enough.'

'Are you going to show me your dress too?'

Kate flushed. 'Your mother insisted. She thought—'

'My mother thought right.'

'She was very kind; she is so beautiful...'

'And you are struggling with her unorthodox relationship with my father.'

'I wouldn't dream of—'

'Everyone else does. My parents' marriage had effectively ended years ago. The pressure to provide an heir took its toll. I suspect they were drifting and probably behind the scenes being *encouraged* towards separation.'

'But they stayed together.'

'Because then *I* happened, after they had given up hope. The only reason divorce would have been sanctioned was the need for an heir, but here I am. Do not look so sad. It is not an unhappy marriage, just different. He does love her, you know, but, as he is fond of saying, what the heart wants...'

'Do you believe that?'

He looked at her before dropping into an armchair in an elegant heap. 'I believe that love is used as an excuse for selfishness among other things. It's been a long day. I could do with a drink.'

'This is a nursery, so there is no bar, but all you have to do is click your fingers and you can have whatever you want, so I'm told.'

'Is that a fact?' he purred, looking at her mouth. The moment of crackling, stomach-quivering tension stretched until he broke it, rising with restless grace to his feet and dragging a hand across his dark hair. 'Sorry, Nanny.'

Kate didn't know what he was apologising for, but she was glad she was no longer subjected to that soul-stripping, truth-drug stare that made her want to tell him what a good kisser he was.

'It doesn't really matter what I believe, does it?'

She didn't say anything even though he glanced her way as though expecting her to argue the point, making her think it was a point he had argued with himself over the years.

'My *mother* believes that Rosa makes my father happy. Their relationship preceded that of my parents but there was never any question of him marrying Rosa. She came from the wrong sort of family. Back then those sorts of things mattered.'

'And they don't now?'

'I don't know what the world's coming to. Non-virgins have even been known to marry into the family.

'The bottom line is my parents are both lovely people and they have a relationship that works for them, but I don't even pretend to understand.'

Freya came in at that moment, an explosion in pink, and as she glowed in response to her father's suggestion she give him a twirl, feeling surplus, Kate made a tactful exit, leaving father and daughter together.

She was in her kitchen making a coffee when the door opened.

'You should lock this. You need your privacy. You're not on duty twenty-four-seven.'

Kate looked at the man whose six-feet-plus frame made the room suddenly very small and arched a brow. 'Most people knock,' she said pointedly. 'And I have been told several times that my predecessor was a saint who hadn't taken a holiday in ten years.'

'Nanny Maeve was pretty much a fixture. People will get used to you. I think they have noticed you already.'

He was looking at her hair and Kate, who was used to people commenting on it, shrugged, thinking that noticing was not the same as accepting.

'Look, I have read the literature and research you sent me and... I've spoken to the professor who has produced the research in the psychology department, and he has arranged an appointment in the education department at the university tomorrow for an assessment for Freya. There is apparently an ongoing research programme and he seemed keen to have Freya take part in it.'

'And how do you feel about that?'

'My daughter is not a guinea pig.'

She studied his rigid jaw and nodded without comment at this understandable response. 'Oh, that's great, well, I mean good that you are taking some action so quickly.'

'And you can't wait to be proved right.'

'That is unfair!' she exclaimed.

His lips compressed as he dragged a hand through his dark hair, creating attractive spikes. Damn her, but she was right, it wasn't. 'Life is not fair, Miss Armstrong. The professor asked me if there was any history of reading problems in the family.'

'Is there?'

'If there was it would have been hidden, to

avoid any suggestion of a taint in the royal blood-line,' he explained with a cynical grimace. 'And Belle's family… I have no idea. The lines of communication, as you are aware, are not open.'

'Couldn't you make the first move?'

'Freya's grandfather lost his right for access when he said that she killed her mother.'

'I'm sure he regrets it…?'

Marco sketched a hard grin. 'I do not regret cutting that bastard out of our lives.'

Kate looked at his flinty eyes and nodded, deciding it was not the moment to push the idea of reconciliation. It would seem that the Prince was not big on forgiveness.

'So tomorrow if you could have Freya ready for ten, under the pretext we will be going… to the beach?'

'Then you will have to go to the beach. You can't promise a child the beach and then change your mind.'

She half expected some push-back but to her surprise none came, just an admonition to remember sunscreen because she was fair-skinned.

The brush of his eyes as he left made her aware of every inch of her pale skin.

'Would you like to take Freya to the playroom while the professor speaks to her father?' The young woman in jeans threw a smile that was several thousand more volts than was appropriate towards Marco, who was shaking hands with the professor who had arrived after his team had completed their tests.

She turned to Freya. 'Would you guys like to go to the playroom while we chat with your daddy, Freya?'

'And then we can go to the beach?' Freya asked Kate.

'Then we can go to the beach,' Kate confirmed.

'I wish I could go too,' the assistant said, only she wasn't looking at Kate and Freya but at Marco, who appeared deep in conversation with the older man.

The young woman might have been showing an unprofessional interest in Marco but her directions were good. They soon found themselves in a sunny playroom.

Freya looked surprised when she saw the other children. She held back for a while, staying close to Kate until a little boy wearing a hearing aid came across and held out a wooden puzzle to her.

'Can I?'

Kate nodded and watched, her heart aching as the solitary little girl responded with growing confidence to the approaches of the other children there.

She didn't really register Marco's presence until he was at her elbow. She rose to her feet, a question in her eyes.

'Well, you will be pleased to hear you have been proved right, they concur with your diagnosis.'

Kate frowned at the direct attack. 'I would have been happy to be proved wrong.'

He pressed the heel of his hand to his forehead and cursed. 'I know, that was…extremely unfair. I should be thanking you. They were very impressed that you had picked up the markers so quickly,' he admitted.

'Apology accepted. Ready to go, Freya,' she yelled.

'Wait a minute!' Marco and Kate watched as she hugged the little boy standing beside her.

'What is she doing?' Marco asked, watching as his daughter waved her hands.

'Signing,' Kate said with a watery smile. 'There is an audiology clinic going on this morning. I think sign language should be taught in all schools; children pick it up so easily.'

'Do you sign?'

'I have the basics.'

Freya reached them, smiling. 'That's my

friend, Simon. He's teaching me how to talk with my hands. Can he come to play some day?'

'I don't see why not, if your papa…?'

'Don't ask me, I'm just the driver,' Marco said drily as they walked to the waiting car, flanked by two cars containing the inevitable security detail.

On the beach, empty but for them, which Kate suspected was not accidental, Kate supervised Freya's application of suncream before she slogged up the slope to a stall selling ice cream. He was not doing much business, so he looked happy when she ordered twenty and he put them in a box for her.

Kate ferried them up to the waiting parked cars and tapped on a blacked-out bulletproof window.

'Thought you might like some ice cream,' she shouted as the window rolled down.

Juggling the three remaining rapidly melting ice creams in her hands, she went back down to the spot where she had left Marco and Freya spreading a blanket on the sand. 'One for you…' Freya snatched the proffered ice cream out of her hand.

'And one…' She switched one ice cream to her free hand.

'That,' Marco observed, nodding to the cars,

'was straight out of my mother's playbook. You trying to win friends?'

Kate flashed him a look. 'Eat it quickly, Freya. It's melting.' She went to hand over one to Marco, holding it at an angle as she licked the melting ice cream off her wrist. 'Oh, my... I'm so sorry.' She giggled as the melting ice cream landed on his immaculate trousers.

From where she stood Freya let out a loud guffaw, Kate's lips quivered, then flattened in shock as her own ice cream made a similar bellyflop and landed in a greasy smear down her front. The child fell about laughing.

'Not so funny now,' Marco said, his mocking voice against her ear sending a shudder through her body.

She dabbed ineffectually at the melting blob, alarm flaring in her eyes as Marco produced a large tissue and approached her. She felt a tiny beat of heat as she visualised his hand against her breast and reacted in panic to stop it happening, snatching it out of his hand with a prim thank you.

'Spoilsport!' he whispered under cover of kneeling down to retrieve a towel. 'Are we going for a swim, Freya?'

'You and me?'

The astonishment in her voice could have been laughable but it wasn't. Marco felt a surge of emotion he could not put a name to, or was too ashamed to.

He could face down a room of critics in dark suits willing him to fall flat on his face and not stumble, not put a foot wrong. His confidence was impregnable, but here on a sandy beach with his own child the things he wanted to say he could find no words for.

And the fact he wanted to say them was all down to Kate. His eyes were sliding to the slim, silent figure when Freya spoke.

Hands set on her skinny hips, his daughter gained his attention as she looked him up and down. 'Papa, you have clothes on.'

His grin made Kate's heart flip.

'Not for long.'

As he stripped off his linen suit and shirt to reveal the pair of black swim-shorts he was wearing underneath Freya was clapping.

Kate's reaction was less enthusiastic, more *visceral*. Her internal temperature had risen several uncomfortable degrees as a shock wave of reaction hit her.

His body was…well, *perfect*. An overused term but in this instance… Long and lean, broad of shoulder and narrow of hips, his legs long and muscular, built for speed and not brute strength. There was not an ounce of excess flesh to disguise the corrugated muscles of his belly or the slabs on his chest.

He made her think of an anatomical diagram of perfect musculature brought to warm, golden, gorgeous, sense-sapping, carnal life.

'Coming, Kate?'

She sat there frozen and shook her head. 'I didn't think, so I forgot my swimsuit,' she improvised, even though it was actually in her bag, and she didn't care if he knew it, there was no way in the world she was changing into it here, in front of him. She felt vulnerable enough as it was without exposing her imperfect body to someone with the most perfect body that ever existed. 'You go and enjoy yourselves.'

'Swim in your pants, Kate. I did when I forgot my swimsuit.'

'Yes, Kate, swim in your pants.'

Her eyes narrowed on his beautiful mocking face. 'Have fun, Freya. I brought a book. Go for your swim and then we should go back. The midday sun is very strong, lethal.'

It wasn't the only thing, she decided, watching as Marco took his daughter's hand and they ran down to the water's edge.

In the car on the way back Freya fell asleep. 'I have a meeting with the educational people next week. Will you come?'

'Of course.'

'They said pretty much what you did. I have let things slide with Freya. I have…that is going to change…she just…'

Kate waited.

'She looks very like her mother.' The guilt tightened its grip on his shoulders. It felt as if he were wearing a lead suit.

The woman he had loved. Kate's heart ached for him. 'That must be hard, not that I know but… I'm sure she has both of you in her, but Freya is her own person.'

'Seeing her today in the playroom… At her fifth birthday there were no children.'

'You were there.'

'No, actually, no, I wasn't. The only reason I remember at all is because there was an intruder that night and I upped security.'

'You could be there for her sixth birthday.'

'I don't like making promises I can't keep, even though I want to. Freya deserves a hands-on father, a loving father,' he said fiercely.

Kate found herself staring at his beautiful hands, her eyes settling on the gold ring. The symbol of what he had lost.

'I think Freya just wants you. And if anyone told me you don't love her, I'd call them an idiot. My dad…' She stopped, an image of her dad appearing in her head, the dad who loved her.

The dad she couldn't forgive. Oh, God, she was an idiot!

'I have sand in my knickers!'

The complaint from the back seat broke the tension in the air and Kate laughed. 'Straight in the bath when we get back, then.'

Marco struggled to focus on the road. Only the image of Kate, in a shower with the water streaming off her lily-pale skin, made him glad to turn into the driveway.

CHAPTER EIGHT

KATE LEANED IN as she applied the finishing touch to her make-up, which was a generous skim of soft pink lip gloss applied with far more precision than she would normally have used.

'Too much?' she asked her reflection of the stranger in the mirror. Some people did this every day but in her view life was too short. She was strictly a flick of mascara, smudge of shadow and smear of gloss kind of girl.

But for special occasions, and she was pretty sure that a ball in a royal palace counted as special, it was good to make the effort. And yes, she was pleased with the results, she decided, turning her face from side to side. She'd skipped a few steps in the online guide to the perfect but subtle party face but the results were pretty good. She quite liked the way the eyeliner emphasised the almond shape of her eyes, and on the third attempt she had nailed the blusher.

As Freya would have said, it was science... or maybe art?

She twirled around on her stool as a small serious voice responded, 'No, not too much. You look...you look shiny.'

'Thank you, Freya.' Kate smiled at the little girl, whose eyes were bright with suppressed excitement.

'Can I put on my dress now, please? I won't spill anything on it again...promise.'

Kate smiled. 'I know you won't, and it was only lemonade, it should be dry now. Ask Julia.'

Her pink robe, adorned with cartoon cats, flapping around her, Freya ran from the room.

Kate slipped off her own robe and laid it on her bed. Her underclothes, which had been bought at a ridiculous price to match her dress, did not cover much. She had passed on the bra-less option, but the strapless silky bra afforded only a token stab at modesty. And the matching silk knickers cut low across her hips and virtually non-existent on her bottom were held together with bits of silk ribbon. They had been designed to incentivise their removal.

Not tonight though, she told herself before her imagination could enter forbidden territory as she shook out the dress and slid down the neatly hidden zip. She ran a hand over the buttery ice-blue fabric and let it slide through her fingers. The other hand remained pressed to her stomach to ease the quivering sensation low in her belly where there was a pack of butterflies running riot.

Kate had smiled at the child's antics, but the truth was she was probably just as excited and apprehensive as Freya, which was stupid. This was just a party. She'd been to parties before. This one was just bigger and involved the odd orchestra and film star. She wasn't even a guest...she was just there as a glorified babysitter.

Admittedly the dress didn't look like one your average babysitter would wear. Reverently she stared at the dress before she wriggled into it. As she reached for the zip she wondered how many times you had to tell yourself you were totally cool before you actually were.

Tomorrow morning, probably, when it was all over.

She practised her cool nanny expression in the mirror and held it about four seconds longer than the last time, before, her heart racing with a mixture of anxiety, excitement took control.

Hardly surprising. Tension was contagious and the palace had been buzzing with it for days, culminating in a general organised mass hysteria today as the final preparations kicked in.

She pushed away the suspicion that the presence of one tall handsome prince might be an extra contributing factor for her. More than the presence of news crews nabbing their spots and doing their soundchecks, or having an entire orchestra stream past her in full evening dress, or hearing the constant buzz of helicopters ferrying guests landing on the lawn.

Looking in the mirror, she adjusted her dress, being assailed by the possibility of a wardrobe malfunction as she visualised the shoestring straps going south and leaving her standing in a pool of silk.

Blinking away the waking-nightmare image, she enjoyed the feel of the silk fabric that hugged her body in all the right places, making the most of her slender curves. She relished the sensuous swish of silk against her legs as she moved, the discreet split in the folds down one side revealing a flash of pale thigh.

Her only jewellery was a pair of amber drop earrings that had been an eighteenth-birthday present from her parents. They'd said the stone was the same colour as her eyes.

Remembering the day brought a fleeting shadow to her eyes, a sadness that a sudden stab of pain offered her an escape from. Tongue between her teeth, she carefully freed the curl that had snagged in one of the butterfly clips behind her ear, carefully untangling it without ruining her hair.

She had weighed up the option between loose or an up-do and in the end settled on a compromise—a *half* up-do, that left her hair long and flowing but showed the delicacy of her facial features and emphasised the slender length of her neck.

Kate was slipping her feet into a pair of satiny high-heeled mules when Freya reappeared, her dimples on show as she tried not to grin. When she saw Kate she clapped.

'Wow, you really will be the belle of the ball!' The maid behind Freya clamped a hand to her mouth. 'Sorry.'

'Julia is right. I'm a princess but you look like a princess tonight.'

'But you are a *real* princess.'

'I have something for you, for your hair.'

Kate was fully anticipating that she'd be offered some plastic hair ornament that she would be obliged to wear, and her smile faded when she saw what Freya was holding.

In the shape of a starburst, the gold hair clip was encrusted with diamonds.

'Oh, Freya, it's beautiful but I couldn't. It's too precious, too valuable.'

'Granny gave it to me for Christmas, it's mine, so I can give it you...or lend it, if you like, for the ball...please, please.'

Responding to the pleading blue eyes, Kate sighed, unable to disappoint the little girl, though the idea of walking around with the princess's jewellery in her hair made her very nervous. 'All right, just for tonight.'

'Julia will put it in for you...sit still,' Freya added.

'Princess bossy,' Kate observed, doing as she was instructed.

'It looks perfect. Come on, Papa is waiting.'

'He is?' Kate's stomach did a double flip. This hadn't been the arrangement as had been relayed to her. 'I thought I was taking you to meet—'

'He's here to escort us.'

Escort you, Kate thought, following the child from the bedroom.

Marco made an unnecessary adjustment to his spotless cuff and continued to pace the room impatiently, unable to control this uncharacteristic restlessness.

The evening would go smoothly. Whatever else Rosa was, she was faultless when it came to organising the big events. She had an eye for detail and delegation.

He did not suffer from stage fright, and the ability to hold his audience was not something he had to work at, but being good at something didn't mean you necessarily liked it. Marco hated working a room and being nice to people that your instinct told you to cross the street to avoid. He'd been smiling for the cameras since he was younger than Freya, wheeled out, hair slicked down for a photo op. There was nothing like the snapshot of a cute kid to distract people from a political scandal or a financial crisis.

Normally he would get through these mind-numbing but necessary social events—necessary in the loosest sense of the word—by anticipating the reward he allowed himself afterwards. The last reward had been a weekend on the Caribbean island that had been a wedding gift for his parents, which they had never to his knowledge visited, in the company of a beautiful corporate lawyer who had a delightfully uninhibited and unemotional attitude to sex.

But there was no naked swimming with a beautiful companion or sundowner cocktails to look forward to this time. He had nothing planned. This oversight likely explained in part the restless tension that he was suffering, that and the fact he had serious doubts about allowing himself to be persuaded to include Freya. His protective instincts were telling him to keep her away from this sort of circus for as long as possible.

Kate Armstrong could give a masterclass in soft power. She'd manipulated him and the hell of it was he had enjoyed it, or at least enjoyed the illicit pain/ pleasure of the forbidden desire he experienced in her company. If it were only in her company, he reflected with a bitter laugh of self-contempt, he might be getting more sleep than he was.

He was starting to think the entire illicit situation was part of the problem—it was the pull of the forbidden pleasure. If he'd slept with her, taking into account his normal game plan, the interlude would by now just be a pleasant memory.

The line was still there, and he was not about to step over it, even if it was slowly driving him mad. It would still be an abuse of a position of power.

A swirl of pink in the periphery of his vision made him turn.

Marco let out a silent whistle, a smile on his lips he picked Freya up and looked beyond her to the figure who had materialised in the doorway. A tremor went through his body, his smile froze. Everything froze. Brain-numbing desire engulfed every cell in his body. If he hadn't been holding his daughter he was sure he would have lunged for her, the need to crush her beautiful mouth under his was so primal, so utterly overwhelming.

That dress… Thinking about the body it covered would cause him serious pain on top of the serious pain he was already enduring. He was starting think he had regressed to his hormonal teens.

'Papa, too tight!'

'Sorry.' Putting his daughter down gave him a chance to claw back some of his self-control. He had not felt this out of control since the day he had jumped into a waterfall head first and been carried down to the rocks below.

People had said it was a miracle he had survived with only a scratch to show for it.

There was no miracle to ground him now, only rigid, hard-fought-for restraint.

He straightened up and the silence stretched and so did Kate's nerves. 'You look very…' She stopped, swallowed and fished around for a description that was not *sublime*.

Which he was.

Tall and commandingly exclusive in perfectly tailored formal attire, his dress shirt creaseless and perfect, the brilliant white emphasising the golden olive of his skin. And with the dark suit hanging off his broad shoulders and emphasising the muscular strength of his long legs, he looked lean and lethal.

'Nice,' she finished lamely.

'Beautiful dress.'

'You paid for it.'

His brows shot up. 'Did I?'

'It was very expensive.'

The confession brought an enigmatic smile. 'Money well spent, I would say. Are we ready, ladies?'

He held out a hand to Freya, who took it, and held out a crooked elbow to Kate, an invitation presumably for her to lay her arm on it.

An innocent enough gesture, and part of her wanted to accept it graciously, but that part of her wanted way too much. Best to avoid physical contact, especially when proximity affected her ability to think coherently.

She made a point of not noticing the invitation instead, moving around to Freya's other side and taking the little girl's other hand in her own.

Mockery shone in his eyes as they challenged her, but Kate tuned him out and turned to Freya.

'A lovely necklace,' she said, touching the delicate silver shell suspended from a chain around the child's neck.

'Papa bought it me.'

Kate looked at *Papa* and immediately regretted it. It took another few moments for her to get her galloping self-control on a leash. This was crazy, and it was going nowhere. He made every woman he looked at feel she was the only woman on the planet. That was the secret of his success. She couldn't allow herself to think otherwise.

'Very pretty.'

'You haven't got a necklace.'

The childish comment brought Marco's eyes to Kate's pearlescent creamy skin. The slender column of her body was immediately under attack from streaks of heat. 'She doesn't need one.'

'I have the lovely hair clip you let me use,' Kate said, struggling with the after-effects of a brief brush with Marco's predatory stare to the extent that it didn't even cross her mind that to the casual observer there might be anything misread in the little procession.

It wasn't until after they had encountered a few uniformed staff that Kate realised that the picture they presented could be easily misinterpreted by someone who didn't know her position in the palace.

This was about the last thing she needed. The way the gossip mill in this place worked, she could only imagine what stories would be circulating by the end of the evening.

They had reached an open area, the stone walls banked with elaborate flower arrangements, when the guests clustered there, awaiting their entrance, parted like a well-dressed sea. The reason soon became obvious. Up ahead she and presumably everyone else could see the King and Queen flanked by a number of high-ranking officials in ceremonial dress heading their way.

She let go of Freya's hand and stepped back, not wanting any part of the prearranged ceremonial procession.

Marco frowningly looked over his shoulder. 'What are you doing?'

She shook her head and said quietly, 'The optics wouldn't look good.' Then, giving Freya a thumbs-up sign, added, 'Have fun and save me a dance.'

Marco nodded, his eyes gleaming dangerously. 'I will.'

Continuing to walk backwards, she blushed. 'I was talking to Freya.'

'*I* was talking to you.' The least he could reward himself with was a chance to hold her in his arms and feel her body against his.

Not in the way he wanted to and it would be a kind of torture probably immediately regretted, but his defiant determination was set in stone.

Kate gave a small, tense smile as his eyes burnt her up. She pressed a hand to the flutter at the base of her throat, almost weeping with relief when she heard a familiar voice at her elbow.

'Going my way?'

It took her a few moments to identify Marco's assistant, who she had met on several occasions now. 'Luca...my, you look smart.'

He looked pleased and twiddled his bow tie, pulling what appeared to be a spare duplicate out of his pocket and admitting with a humorous grin, 'Couldn't tie it. Someone lent me a clip-on.'

'I couldn't tell,' she promised.

'God, I could do with sunglasses,' Kate murmured as they slipped into the ballroom through one of the side entrances. Between the chandeliers suspended from the high vaulted ceiling covered in frescoes and the jewellery the female guests were wearing it was a real bling fest. 'I suddenly feel quite underdressed,' she admitted, taking a glass of champagne from a passing waiter.

'You look fabulous,' the young man said with such sincerity that she might have been flattered if she hadn't been able to see he was checking out the crowd for someone. She watched him with a smile for a moment, wondering if he'd been tasked to look after her, before taking pity on him.

'I suppose we should mingle. See you later.'

He vanished so fast that she almost laughed. Instead, she exchanged her empty glass for a second one, which would usually be her last. She knew her limit but, seized by uncharacteristic recklessness, she found herself wishing that she were in a position to go over it...a long way... However, drunk in charge of a child would not look good on her résumé.

Kate was nursing the second glass when a hush of expectation fell over the room, the lights dimmed, all but the ones on the grand sweeping staircase as the orchestra began to play the national anthem.

The King and Queen appeared at the top of the stairs and began their ascent with suitably regal majesty, the Queen wearing a tiara that put any other jewel in the place in the shade. But it was the couple behind that Kate was watching as the camera bulbs flashed.

Her heart twisted in her chest as she watched Freya, in her pretty pink frothy dress, pick her way down the steps in her embroidered pink slippers, glancing up after every other step up for reassurance from the tall man who held her hand.

That Marco looked simply magnificent was a given. He made every man in the room look like a pale imitation, but it was the fact the world could see the pride on his face and the words of encouragement he was mouthing to Freya that brought tears to Kate's eyes.

She wasn't the only one who was moved, she suspected.

The photos would be guaranteed international front-page coverage.

If she'd seen the photos without having any insight, she might have viewed any photo spread with a degree of cynicism and she'd have been wrong. Wrong about how much else? she wondered.

She was in a position now to know that first impressions would be wrong. This was no PR stunt.

Instincts were not always right. There was sometimes a back story that changed the narrative. Had she even considered her parents' narrative...?

She had not given her parents a chance to

offer their viewpoint. She had made no effort to see things from where they had been standing. She'd been too hurt, too eager to condemn without question. Kate felt her grip on the high ground slip as the infectious germ of doubt took up residence in her head while the orchestra struck up the chords of a Strauss waltz. With her inside information Kate had known they would.

She had walked through the steps with Freya all week and the little girl had them nailed, so long as nerves didn't get in the way.

Kate watched, willing Freya on as the couples circled the floor, the King and Queen giving a practised performance. But all eyes were on the little girl and her father.

As if he sensed her gaze across the room, Marco's eyes found hers. Tension slid down her spine, the people, the music all seemed to fade and grew fuzzy until Kate's entire world narrowed to his bold silver stare. She didn't even register the music stopping. It was the applause from the guests around her that shook Kate free of the spell that gripped her.

Real or imagined, she was shaken by the effect of the silent communication across the room. She watched as Marco took Freya to stand with his parents and walked back to the raised dais where there was a microphone.

It was clear immediately that Marco was as adept at public speaking as he seemed to be at everything else. Of course, it helped that his deep vibrant voice could have made a grocery list sound interesting.

He had his audience from the first introduction line as he issued the anticipated congratulations to his parents on their special day and spoke of duty and the unity that was the strength of the country and its people.

The real news he couched as an afterthought wrapped inside his deep gratitude to the forward-thinking royal council for their wisdom in proposing a change to the outdated rule that gave males precedence over females, thus altering the royal line of succession in a way that made it fairer.

At least she wasn't the only one who found his voice hypnotic, Kate thought as the room exploded into applause that was not polite but spontaneous. It lasted while Marco, after producing a charming smile of thanks, walked across to join the rest of his family.

Kate watched Freya, who was clapping non-stop as her father reached them. A smile tugged at her lips. It was amazing how the child's confidence had grown in such a short space of time. She was as easy to love as her rather less huggable father was to… As her eyes drifted to the tall dynamic figure, Kate's thoughts skittered to a halt. She sensed that if she allowed them to run free for another moment there was something *looming*, an answer to a question she had not even asked herself yet.

The thought of the question panicked her so thoroughly that when a man who addressed his invitation to her cleavage, not her face, asked her to dance, she couldn't think of a plausible reason to say no.

'I have just been telling Freya that one day she will be Queen, but she is more interested in teaching your mother how to salsa...' The King lowered his voice. 'Is salsa an appropriate dance to be teaching a child of Freya's age, Marco? This new nanny...is she working out, do you think?'

Marco opened his mouth and closed it again as he caught sight of the top of a red head on the dance floor, his eyes narrowing as he struggled to identify her partner. The tension in his features relaxing when he recognised a married courtier whose wife was rumoured to keep him on a short leash.

'She is well qualified. I doubt if we could keep her even if we wanted to.' And he wanted, he wanted Kate Armstrong. His mind knew it was a bad idea, but his body didn't care, his body wanted Kate Armstrong, and he wanted to find the oblivion he craved deep in her warm body.

'Oh, well, Freya seems…less tongue-tied at least, which is a good thing. And you must be pleased with yourself. There's no backing out now, is there?' the King observed with a chuckle. 'I must say tonight is a great success, thanks in large part to Rosa… I always enjoy these occasions.' He looked at his tall son curiously. 'Unlike you?'

'Does it show?' Marco asked, flicking an invisible speck from his lapel as he watched Kate circle the floor.

'Not at all. You're very good at the diplomacy, you could always leave early…?'

Marco laughed at the suggestion. 'Your concern is appreciated but what do you suggest, Father, I get a headache…?' Marco excused himself and walked across to where an animated Freya was chattering to her grandmother.

'Having fun?'

'Yes, Papa, I think that lady over there is waving to you.'

Marco turned his head to follow her finger and identified the tall blonde who was waving to catch his attention. It took him a moment longer to recall her name.

Kate's polite smile was wearing thin. Her dance partner had stepped on her toes again.

'Did I mention my wife couldn't come tonight? Her sister is ill. I'm fending for myself.'

No, she thought, you were too busy telling me what an important person you are.

'Oh, what a shame,' she said, matching his sincerity while watching as a tall blonde on the other side of the room, in a dress that she just had to have been sewn into, placed a proprietorial hand on Marco's arm as he leaned in to hear what she was saying.

Kate knew who she was because she had looked her up in relation to the gossip. Out of curiosity, she had told herself, as she was telling herself now that the shaft of pain that felt like a knife sliding between her ribs was because she'd skipped lunch.

The leaning in, the dark head next to the blonde head—the imaginary knife twisted. Kate stumbled and saw her partner wince.

'You trod on my foot!' he exclaimed, sounding outraged.

After the trampling her poor toes had suffered she thought this hardly redressed the balance, but she settled for a meek and diplomatic apology. 'So…sorry.'

'My wife is a very good dancer.'

There was a plus side. His clammy hand no longer strayed down to her bottom. Things got even better when he developed a limp and excused himself.

'Jackie, you're looking good.'

'Don't worry, darling, I'm not stalking you. I'm here as a plus one.'

The guest list was not something that Marco took a personal interest in. Any specific requests would have come from his office.

Too tired to respond to her flirtatious laughter, Marco found himself wondering how he had ever thought the fake sounded amusing.

'I can see you're sceptical.'

He wasn't interested enough in the conversation to be sceptical, but he could definitely feel boredom setting in.

'But seriously,' he heard her say. 'Lawrence… I'm his plus one…was hoping you could take a meeting…? There are rumours of an airport expansion and you know he is—'

'I know who Lawrence Milton is, but the answer is no because there will be no airport expansion, so I can save you the softening-up process.'

The model's smile was tight. 'Oh, I told him you don't "soften up" *and* my influence was only ever limited.'

Non-existent would have been more accurate but Marco let it pass.

'But I thought I'd give it a try...?'

'No expansion.' Aside from the green issues, bringing in more tourists would despoil the very things that attracted visitors.

It was all about balance.

'Oh, well, thank you for the heads-up...' A half wistful expression crossed the model's beautifully made-up face. 'We had fun didn't we...?'

Marco raised a brow. 'Sentimental? That's not like you.'

She shrugged. 'We all change. You have.'

Marco bent in to kiss her cheek, barely registering the comment as he moved away, his eyes scanning the crowd for a distinctive redhead.

In her search for Freya, Kate noticed the dance floor had emptied. She soon discovered why. Her shy charge, who had discovered her inner diva, was there, taking centre stage, partnered by her grandfather.

As the last chords played Freya curtsied to the King before clapping herself.

Guests' cameras were banned and the palace censored any releases from the official photographers and film crews present, but if that image got out it would capture the hearts of millions. Kate, who knew that despite his multiple faults Marco was all about the best interests of his child, suspected it wouldn't.

An ebullient Freya spotted Kate and came running over, pushing her way through the crowds and effectively putting all curious eyes on her nanny, an identity that she heard pronounced on all sides as Freya pulled her onto the floor for their dance.

Kate recognised the child was over-wound and overtired, *over* being the operative word at the moment the normally sweetly biddable child showed a marked inclination to pout when thwarted. Kate knew that she just as easily become tearful.

I've created a monster, Kate thought with fond amusement. There was definitely more of Freya's father in her than she had realised, watching as the little girl imperiously demanded a *'salsa if you know one'* from the indulgent conductor.

A ripple of laughter went around the room as the salsa beat, backed by a full orchestra, pumped out.

'You promised,' Freya reminded Kate. The

bright cheeks and glitter in her eyes had all the hallmarks of exhaustion as she held out her hands and showed a strong inclination to sulk.

'One dance and then you say goodnight.'

Freya looked inclined to argue but after a moment, much to Kate's relief, she nodded and sighed. The last thing Kate wanted to cope with was a childish meltdown in front of the several hundred VIP pairs of eyes.

'OK.'

As couples joined them on the dance floor and she gently pushed the child through the series of moves they had been practising as a pre-bedtime treat, Kate's eyes were drawn to a laughing young couple sealed at the hip, moving in unison as they swayed sinuously to the music with practised show-stopper ease.

What would it feel like to dance this one with Marco? To move to the beat with their bodies sealed? She pushed the image away but not before her body reacted feverishly to the imaginary scenario.

After the dance ended and before Freya could make the inevitable plea for just one more, Kate scanned the room but failed to locate Marco. It wasn't as if he blended in with the crowd. Nor could she see the beautiful blonde model. *What a coincidence*, she thought sourly.

She looked at Freya's too bright, overtired eyes and pale face and made a unilateral decision, which was what she was being paid for.

'Let's go and say goodnight,' she said, placing a hand on the child's shoulders and guiding Freya across to where the King and Queen were watching the proceedings in the company of a select few.

Rosa, who had organised the entire event, was not one of them. At least the King did not rub his wife's nose in it publicly.

Marco struggled and failed to hide his frustrated response to the interruption.

'Yes?' Like all his team, the head of security was dressed to blend in. He didn't, but then that was not necessarily a bad thing.

'Can you not deal with it?' Whatever the 'it' was, he already knew the answer. The man had ten years' special forces experience. If he couldn't deal with it, Marco wouldn't stand an earthly chance.

'I could, as I told His Majesty, but the message came back and he has requested that you personally...'

Marco sighed. 'What is it?' he asked with forced calm. You didn't question a royal command, at least not in public.

'A helicopter has strayed into the no-fly

zone… It's not an issue, our intel suggests just an opportunist film crew, and we have two of our choppers escorting them into the airport as we speak.'

'It sounds like you are on top of it. So what does my father expect me to do?'

'As to that, Highness, I have no idea, but the message I received was that he wanted you to—'

Across the room the King caught Marco's eye, tipped his head and tapped the side of his nose in a secret-shared attitude.

Marco heaved out a sigh of understanding. Now it made sense! His father had decided to don the mantle of an unlikely fairy godmother, in a 'you will *leave* the ball early' sense.

The request was his legitimate headache, get-out-of-jail excuse; the irony was that on any previous occasion he wouldn't have needed asking twice.

'Fine,' he sighed out, clinging by the skin of his teeth to his sense of irony. With a well-meaning father like his, who needed anarchists to spoil your plans? 'A royal command? What can you say? Lead the way.'

Despite her previous vow not to curtsey, Kate found herself doing just that, or at least a modified version, when she came face to face with the King. Did size matter, curtsey-wise?

Kate had been prepared to dislike him but, like his wife, he actually came across as very approachable, a lot less daunting in reality than his son, though she suspected that Freya's presence helped. It was hard to be standoffish when a five-year-old was declaring herself bored, but at least she managed to get through the ordeal of introduction without saying anything controversial.

'Where's Papa?' Freya sulked as she got into bed, protesting she wasn't even slightly tired.

'I don't know.' Kate had her dark suspicions, though, and all of them involved a blonde with endless legs. 'How about you just close your eyes and if you're still awake in a bit you can have a story?' she suggested, switching on the night light before she switched off the main light in the room.

'I won't fall asleep,' the child asserted confidently.

Kate smiled and brushed the hair off her warm forehead before quietly moving around the room, picking up the clothes that had been dropped on the floor. By the time she left Freya was sleeping deeply.

Moving back to her own apartment, switching off the lights behind her as she went, Kate was pretty sure that she wouldn't be able to follow suit. Her thoughts were still racing, the sights and sounds of the glittering evening a confusing blur, but most disturbing was the imprint scorched into her brain of Marco's face as he had stared at her. The fierce, scorching intensity still making her stomach flutter now, and feeding her restlessness.

The party would still be going on, though Marco, his duty done, might have taken his party somewhere more private by now, she thought, feeding her misery with the masochistic imagined scene of seduction. Which was ridiculous because she already knew what his lifestyle was, it was just that seeing him in action tonight had brought it home.

She'd seen him at work and he was good, very good. Was he as good at play? wondered that little voice in her head—the one that enjoyed picking at an unhealed wound.

Except she wasn't wounded, she was just thinking of someone having meaningless sex with her boss. She didn't envy her one bit. She had decided a long time ago that she didn't want meaningless sex, she wanted something deeper, more meaningful.

'And Kate never changes her mind about anything.'

Her delicate jaw quivered and her eyes filled with tears as she heard her brother's voice in her head.

The accusation might have been true once, but in the short time she'd been here Kate knew she had changed. Her preconceptions had been challenged, not just by Marco, but by the feelings he had shaken loose in her.

She considered her options. A long relaxing soak in the bath, or slipping between crisp sheets and falling into a deep sleep? Both excellent options had she not known that there was zero chance of relaxation or sleep, deep or otherwise.

The evening scent of flowers blowing in through the open window suggested another option. Sliding her feet back into her shoes, she winced, the pressure on the balls of her feet burning.

She sat down and checked out her feet, relieved to see they were not blistered, but she definitely wouldn't be squeezing into any heels for the next few days. In fact, why bother at all? she asked herself rebelliously. The idea of damp grass on her bare feet was actually rather appealing.

CHAPTER NINE

ALTHOUGH MARCO WAS ninety-nine per cent sure that his father's command that he accompany the security detail to the airport was a ruse to provide him with an excuse to absent himself from the ball, there had been the one per cent possibility there was a legitimate reason for his presence.

This possibility quickly vanished; his royal presence was actually a hindrance to the men who knew their jobs. Marco only stayed long enough to have his suspicions confirmed, before bagging a car to drive himself back from the airport.

He'd learnt to drive in a similar open-sided soft-top Jeep. He smiled to himself as he negotiated the white-knuckle bends of the coastal road, remembering the days when being grounded for taking the off-roader onto a road, and practising his behind-the-wheel skills on this very stretch, had got him grounded.

Grounded, the worst thing in the world that, to his resentful teenage mind, could happen. *Dio*, he felt quite nostalgic for those lost days as he accelerated smoothly out of a bend in a way that only someone who knew the road like the back of his hand could.

How did life get so damned complicated?

Complications, he mused, thinking of Kate Armstrong dressed in that blue dress looking... The woman had taken up residence in his head. His had not been the only eyes following her, the only eyes admiring her fresh beauty, her glorious hair.

He didn't want her in his head. He wanted her in his bed—you couldn't get much more simple than that. He was actually creating complications where there weren't any.

And any rules he'd be breaking were of his own making. Couldn't he *unmake* them?

The party was still in full swing when he slipped back into the palace through the kitchen. He got as far as one of the corridors leading off it. This corridor was lined with cool rooms, tonight acting as a rat-run for wait staff, who stared at him and, when he stopped dead, diverted around him.

They were probably wondering what he was doing, and now Marco was asking the same question of himself. What *was* he doing? He'd been gifted his get-out-of-jail-free card by his father. Only a masochist, a madman or someone who actually enjoyed small talk, which was the same thing, would walk back into his cell and lock the door behind him.

So instead he retraced his steps, on impulse snatching a bottle of champagne from a cooler containing dozens, and headed out into the night.

He knew where he was heading but he didn't acknowledge it even to himself. Only when he reached his destination did he admit that it was not by accident.

It was by *need*.

He allowed himself to relive that sizzling moment of eye contact when all the pretence had been peeled away. He had to do something about it… Two people who wanted sex should be a straightforward thing, and to hell with the consequences, mocked the voice in his head. *Very mature.*

The simple pleasures, Kate thought with a sigh as she enjoyed the squish of the cool grass between her toes, were underrated. She rubbed her upper arms as a cooling breeze all the way from the ocean made her shiver. She found herself at one of the viewpoints scattered around the grounds. This one the nearest to the nursery wing. Eyes trained on the ocean, a dark strip beyond the glitter of the illuminated walled city of St Boniface.

A dark strip that represented miles and miles of emptiness…vast. And…she slowed her breathing, trying to emulate that emptiness, conscious of the tension loosening its grip on her body.

When she closed her eyes could she hear music or was it simply the gentle breeze in the trees? She didn't care as she let herself sway to an invisible rhythm, her dress floating around her as she dipped and whirled, head back, eyes closed. At the end of the silent melody she paused and curtsied to the invisible audience until she realised it wasn't invisible, at which point she pulled herself upright in a jerky motion, and, heart pounding, faced her audience of one.

'What are you doing here?' she snapped spikily, thinking goodbye relaxation, goodbye common sense.

'I live here. That was very pretty.' But she was not pretty. She was *beautiful*, and never more so than at that moment. He ate up the visual, committing to memory her eyes, enormous in the pale oval of her face, as she stood there looking like some sort of sexy sacrificial virgin in that dress.

Then he saw her feet and a slow smile spread across his lean face.

'To lose one shoe, Cinders, could be considered a misfortune, but to lose two…?'

She responded to his taunt with a defensive, 'I haven't lost them. I know exactly where they are.'

Pity the same could not be said of my mind, Kate mused despairingly as she struggled to remove her hungry stare from his mouth. *When was the last time I actually felt in control of my life…?* At least when she had arrived she had still had the security of knowing what was right and wrong. Now exposure to this man had blown that out of the water.

It was wrong to want him, but she did. Did that mean she was wrong about other things too?

Feelings she hadn't known she possessed had been awoken and they hurt. The constant confusion, the constant questioning, the constant yearning that made her *feel*… Feel as if she were walking on the edge of a cliff. She glanced towards a very real cliff in the distance. It didn't seem nearly as precarious as the one she was balancing on.

No wonder her nerves were shredded.

'Have you come to say goodnight to Freya?' she asked, thinking, *Have you come straight from the blonde's bed?* A question that came straight from her newly discovered jealous streak.

She silently listed the reasons she shouldn't feel jealous: firstly she had no right, and secondly... Actually, firstly was enough.

'I'm afraid she's asleep.'

'As all good girls should be at this hour...' he drawled, his voice dropping a seductive octave as he delivered a skin-tingling, 'Are you a good girl, Cinders...?'

Kate moistened her lips and swallowed, fighting the childish impulse to cover her ears to cut out the insidious sound of his beautiful voice, all honey warmth and sinful suggestion.

'I am not a *girl*, I'm a woman, and it will be a cold day in hell...' She paused, discarding the analogy. No analogy was strong enough to convey how much she *didn't* need a prince to save her. A miracle...now that was different. If there were one of those on offer she'd definitely be a taker!

Shaking her head, she walked over to a gentle mound in the grassy expanse some feet away from where he stood and sat down, her eyes directed at the distant sea view. Regaining that little window of peace she had enjoyed was, she suspected, a non-starter, but at least it was breathing space.

After a pause, Marco came over to where she sat. 'Can I join you?'

'It's a free country,' she retorted childishly, and then sighed because it was *his* country. Lucky his shoulders were broad because the idea of that much responsibility was daunting in theory, but for him it was a reality.

She stared ahead, resisting the temptation to turn her head when her tingling senses told her he had come to sit beside her, not close enough to shift her defences into the red-alert zone, but enough to make her...twitchy.

'I was just getting some fresh air,' she said when the silence became unbearable.

'Me too.' He held up the bottle he carried, tilting the tip before, with an expert twist and a gentle pop, he released the fizz.

'You've done that before.'

'Like to join me in a toast?'

'To what?' she asked, feeling as though this conversation of nothing was just a prelude... *Or foreplay*, suggested the voice in her head.

What she knew about foreplay could be written on a postage stamp.

'To fresh air?' he suggested, his eyes going

from the bottle to her face. Confessing with a lopsided smile, 'I haven't got two glasses. In fact, I haven't got one.'

Something about him, the reckless combustible quality in his attitude, made her wonder if this was his first bottle.

'No, I haven't even had a sip,' he said, responding to her unspoken question. 'There we go!' He held the bottle like a trophy, before lifting it to his lips and taking two deep gulps. 'Waste not want not, is that not what you say?'

She responded to the challenge in his eyes by snatching the bottle off him and taking a large swallow, rather spoiling the effect when she choked.

'Not your first...?' he suggested, taking it back.

'I had two glasses, my limit,' she admitted.

Their eyes connected. 'So, you are playing dangerously tonight?'

A little shiver went down her spine as she veiled her eyes with her lashes. 'I'm not the type.' But there were times when she wished she were.

He took another swallow. 'Who told you that, *cara*...?' he drawled.

'I was always the sensible one at home. Jake was the emotional, reckless one.' She laughed, suddenly realising that the roles had been reversed.

'What's the joke?'

'Me?'

He arched a brow but didn't say anything as he lifted the bottle to his lips. Kate watched his brown throat work as he swallowed and felt a stab of pure lust. He put the bottle on the ground and turned his head. Caught looking, she lifted her chin, refusing to lower her gaze.

She managed to maintain eye contact for seconds until the heat in his gaze, the quickening in her blood, got too frightening. She had never felt this way, never imagined feeling this way.

For a while they sat side by side not saying anything. She'd heard of companionable silence, but this one was not. It was *dangerous* silence. It made Kate think of a pile of dry tinder waiting for a spark, and yet, despite the tension in the darkness and silence, she felt a strange connection to the man beside her.

Kate shook her head, swallowing to alleviate the dryness in her throat before she skimmed her lips quickly with the tip of her tongue.

'Tonight went well...you must be pleased.' Her voice sounded high and forced even to her own ears.

'Have I done the right thing...?' he wondered out loud. 'Or will one day my daughter curse me? You know, I never even considered that possibility. That she might not *want* to be Queen. That it is more a curse than a gift. It was a battle and I won...' The last self-condemnatory insight was muttered half to himself.

'Freya could always walk away. You could have walked away if you had wanted to.'

He turned and looked at her, a series of expressions drifting across his face. 'I suppose I could have but it never occurred to me. Duty is not an optional extra. I never fought against it, it's more like I filtered it out. Like the bodyguards, you stop noticing them.'

Kate, who felt hideously conscious of the men with guns, could not imagine that ever being true.

He saw her expression and grinned. 'It's different for me. I've always lived under a microscope. My actions always judged. I don't want to make it sound like I'm a victim. I'm not. I lead a very privileged life. I have freedom.'

'There was no pressure for an arranged marriage like your parents.'

'My parents' marriage was not arranged.'

'Oh, sorry. I just assumed...'

'Because my father keeps a mistress and my

mother pretends not to notice? Yeah, I can see how you would… But no, my parents were a *love* match.' The sneer in his voice was overt. 'It was quite a scandal at the time. They were both being *encouraged* to marry other people, but people fall out of love.'

And he had thought, in his arrogance, that he had avoided the trap his parents had fallen into. If you were never in love you couldn't fall out of love. There was a lot less pain and humiliation involved in a loveless marriage. The destructive power of love had had the last laugh.

'Your father…the King…he was very polite when…'

'He is always polite. If there is anything that appears unpleasant, my mother ignores it. On paper they are the perfect couple.' On paper he and Belle had been the perfect couple.

'He looks just like his photos, very *noble*. Did you have a mistress when you…?' Her hand went to her mouth as she looked at him, her eyes wide and horrified. 'I am so sorry, that was…'

'No, it's a legitimate question, but no, I didn't. That is not to say I wouldn't have at some stage,' he observed, self-contempt in his voice. 'Not much like your parents' marriage, I suppose.'

She gave an odd little laugh. 'My parents' marriage? I don't even know if they had one…a marriage, that is. I don't know who my parents were…are…but my mum and dad love one another. Well, I always thought they did, but then I always thought that they were my parents. I always thought I knew…' Her voice cracked.

'I don't know why I'm telling you this. Oh, God, it's so embarrassing. I really hate crying,' she gritted as she dropped her head to her chest, hiding behind the veil of flaming hair, chest heaving as she fought to contain the emotions that were leaking out of her.

Marco had been an objective observer to many tears, the majority of these calculated displays aimed at eliciting a reaction in him. The only thing they left was a nasty taste in his mouth. He dealt with these types of situations by removing himself from the scene.

Watching Kate declare her utter contempt for her tears of genuine emotion, he felt no urge to walk away, he felt an alien urge to comfort her, but his utter cluelessness of how to go about this left him feeling unaccustomedly helpless.

Lust was normally a lot simpler than this.

Walking away from uncomfortable situations a lot easier too.

Placing a thumb under her chin, he tipped her face up to his and he looked into her swimming eyes. How could a person be so tough and self-sufficient and so vulnerable at the same time? A vulnerability he could see she hated owning.

'I can see why you hate it; you look terrible.' She actually looked breathtakingly beautiful.

Kate looked at him for a moment, her amber eyes shining with indignation before she laughed at herself. 'I can be so ridiculous sometimes.'

He grinned back. 'That's better, and you're telling me because I asked.' Which was not keeping things simple. His motivation remained something of a mystery to him, unless the answer was as simple as that he simply wanted to know.

'So you discovered you were adopted recently?'

She nodded. 'My gran died.' As she began to explain the sequence of events, she realised that it was a relief. After all the weeks of bottling it up, sharing her story was cathartic, even though the recipient of her confidences was the last person she would have expected to choose. 'At least, I *thought* she was my gran. I was helping go through her papers, and I discovered our adoption papers. Discovered my entire life has been a lie. Everything changed.'

'So you and your brother—older or younger?'

'A year older.'

'You're both adopted. How did he take it?'

'He already knew.' Hurt quivered in her voice. 'He's known for years, and he didn't tell me. I thought we were so close and *he* was angry with *me*. Jake thinks I was punishing our mum and dad.'

'Are you?'

She opened her mouth to angrily deny it, and then closed it, shaking her head. 'Maybe a little,' she confessed. 'But I suddenly didn't know how to act around them. It felt surreal. Why didn't I sense it? Don't people sense these sorts of things? I think Jake did. He went looking for proof of his suspicions…went looking for his birth parents. But his mother is dead and his father has another family and didn't want to know him.'

'Poor guy. Maybe your brother wanted to save you from that.'

'I don't need saving or protecting!' she

flared. 'I am more than capable of looking after myself.'

'All right, maybe they, your mum and dad, were the ones who were afraid? Maybe they were uncomfortable about telling you, and every day they didn't just compounded their guilt? I don't know, why don't you ask them?'

'I can't even talk to them. They lied.' Even she could hear the doubt in her voice.

'They messed up, but people do that every day of the week. Do you want to know who your birth parents were?'

'No. They didn't want me, why would I look for them?' She shook her head and angled a confused look at his face. 'I really don't know why I'm telling *you* this.'

'Maybe because of my warm, understanding personality…no…? Ah, well, maybe I just happened to be there when you had, what do they call it, a trigger moment?' He picked up the empty bottle, his lips quirking as he shook it and looked at her with eyes dark enough to get lost in. 'Or possibly…?' he mocked.

'If that were the case *you* would be telling *me* your deepest darkest secrets. I only had a mouthful.'

'Oh, the night is young yet, *cara*,' he teased. 'You might unlock my secrets yet.'

'It isn't…young, that is, the night,' she realised, catching sight of the face of the thin-banded watch he was wearing.

'Hold on, Cinders,' he said, catching her arm as she went to get to her feet. 'I haven't had my promised dance yet.'

Kate subsided again, her skin tingling not just where his fingers had lain but all over. She felt the dark scratch under every inch of her body.

'Be serious,' she said, trying to sound exasperated and missing by a mile.

'I am deadly serious. Always,' he said, straight-faced, the gleam in his dark eyes making her stomach flip.

'When you've just drunk a bottle of champagne?'

He grinned and, rising in one fluid motion, dragged her with him. 'It might have taken the edge off, but no, I am not drunk. Dance with me.' He took hold of both of her hands and performed an artistic flamenco stamp.

'There is no music,' she countered, struggling to inject some sanity into this increasingly surreal conversation.

'A mere technicality.' He put one of her hands on his shoulder, then the second, before placing his on her waist.

'Are you off your meds?' she pushed out, drawing a deep growl of laughter from him.

There was no corresponding laughter in his eyes. They were darkly focused...relentless.

Kate's chest heaved as she fought to compensate for the fact she'd forgotten to breathe. What she really needed was air between them, space. His proximity was doing terrible things to her nervous system. As for professional distance...the ache at the damp apex of her legs was not professional.

'You are quite beautiful.'

She wrinkled her nose, her eyes sliding from his. 'I'll take that as a yes, then.'

'You are the strangest woman I have ever met, full of contradictions.'

'Sure, I'm a real enigma,' she muttered, fighting the urge to follow him and losing as he began to move. He was actually a good dancer, but then he was one of those tedious people who were good at everything, she told herself, trying to feel scorn or even resentment but it wouldn't come. Instead her thoughts moved dangerously on to all the *other* things he might be good at.

He'd had very good reviews and even allowing for exaggeration... *Did she want to find out?*

'There, you can hear it now too.'

'No,' she said, fighting hard to retain a grip.

But, as if pre-programmed, her body had started to follow his lead.

One hand placed, long fingers spread, in the small of her back, his hooded eyes darkened as she responded to the slightest of increases in pressure. Stepping into him until they were so close there was no oxygen between them.

Kate made a conscious effort to breathe, focus, afraid she might forget and fall in a dead faint at his feet. He was all warmth and solid slabs of muscle.

Her skin prickled, her insides dissolved, her heart climbed into her throat, the spreading tingle of excitement igniting and spreading across the surface of her skin, the sensation as though she had woken up from a dream to discover it wasn't a dream, it was real.

Desire pumping through his body in a steady logic-destroying stream, he held her eyes with his bold black hypnotic stare. Watching her face as he ground the bold imprint of his erection against the softness of her belly, watching with a smile of predatory pleasure her pupils eat up the gold.

His action drew a shocked gasp from Kate as she felt the heat between them reach scalding point. The air around them seemed to shimmer with the combustion they were creating. Shimmer with the passion that burned away any sense of self-preservation she might have retained. She was deep, *deep*, and lost inside to-hell-with-the-consequences territory.

She watched, her eyelids heavy, the ache between her legs throbbing, and as his sensuous mouth came down she stretched up, greedy for the contact. When it came, the slow, sensuous, skilled seduction of his mouth just fed the urgency building inside her. She wanted more. The passion was like nothing she had ever experienced, nothing she had ever dreamed existed.

He bit into the lush softness of her lower lip, sliding his tongue into her mouth, as they continued to drift around. Moving in slow, lazy, ever-decreasing circles until they were not moving at all.

Her curves had automatically acclimated themselves into his hard angles, their bodies sealed. Her entire body quivered with the expectation of what happened next. They were standing still, Kate's head tilted, her hands cushioned between them, pressed flat against the hard barrier of his chest. Everything locked, including their eyes.

He traced the angle of her jaw and ran his fingers down the extended column of her creamy neck, brushing his lips against the blue-veined pulse point before he kissed her as though he wanted to drain her. Fine tremors ran through his powerful body, as if the effort to contain the need and hunger driving him was making him shake.

'I want to take your clothes off,' he purred throatily. 'I want to see you, touch you… I want to be inside you, *cara*, I want to have you hold me there all night.'

His teasing words made her whimper, made the wet core of her sex ache as she rubbed her body against him, while she struggled to get any words past the occlusion in her throat.

'Not here…'

He looked at her face, the driven need in his drawing the golden skin tight against his marvellous bones, and nodded, then, without a word, scooped her up into his arms and strode off towards the building.

To the victor goes the spoils.

The words drifted through her head, except this was not a war and there was not some unwilling prize…victim. She was an eager partner in this seduction.

They encountered no one on their way to her flat. She was past caring if they had. She kissed him, their hot breaths mingling, as he collided with the wall and items of furniture along the way.

Marco put her on her feet beside her bed and as she stood there shivering, not with cold but with the need that was sweeping through her, he left her side to turn the big key in the lock, turning at the last moment.

'I have no discovery fantasies...unless you do?'

The lines fanning out from his eyes deepened as he watched her eyes go round with horror at the idea of someone walking in on them.

'I've always thought if you were doing it properly you wouldn't notice. Don't worry. I have other fantasies though, always happy to share,' he rasped wickedly as he came back to join her. Then, leaning in close to kiss her, he whispered against her lips, 'Do you have fantasies, Kate?'

She responded with the simple truth. 'You're my fantasy.'

He said something in Italian, the stark hissed meaning pretty clear as, holding her eyes, he reached for the zip on her dress, sliding it all the way down. She shivered as his fingers, cool against her own, moved over heated skin, brushed the flesh in the small of her back, spreading out across the curve of her tight bottom.

His eyes only left hers when he slid the thin straps over the curve of her smooth shoulders and watched the dress fall to the ground at her feet in a silken heap.

Standing there in the strapless bra and pants, she felt a flurry of uncertainty. Her toes curled and her hands clenched as the silence stretched. Was he shocked by her skinniness, the jutting bones, the lack of curves, not at all what he had been used to?

'You are even more beautiful than I imagined and I've been imagining since the first moment I saw you. These are very pretty,' he purred, sliding a teasing clever finger under the silk of her bra, causing her nipples to instantly pucker and harden painfully.

The intensity of his stare made things shift deep inside and fed the increasingly urgent signals zinging between her nerve endings.

'You are so sensitive,' he observed with gloating approval. 'I *need* your skin,' he growled throatily as he trailed a kiss over the gentle curve of her cleavage before peeling back the bra cups and allowing his eyes to feast on the perfect oval mounds of coral-tipped flesh. While he was unclipping her bra he bent his head to suckle and tease the hardened peak into even more aching prominence, sending shards of pleasure through Kate's body as she arched her back, her fingers sliding into his thick pelt of hair to hold him against her as she squirmed against him and began to pull at his clothes, frustrated beyond reason by the layers separating them.

He absorbed the softness of her body like a man finding water in the desert.

Her eager hands were clutching everywhere, not slickly, but desperate and clumsy, tearing a button, clutching at his behind, digging in, her breath coming in a series of uneven gasps and sighs.

Marco felt as if he were in an inferno. He had never wanted a woman the way he wanted Kate, never experienced this elemental level of need, a need that involved every nerve ending, every fibre.

She finally found some skin and pressed her lips to the golden section of chest, finding his pebble-hard nipple, his deep, almost animal groan shocking and exciting her, filling her with a sense of glorious female power she had never experienced before.

The primal emotions ripping through her made her knees shake and then it didn't matter because she was on her back on the bed and he was peeling the silk knickers down her thighs.

He stared at her body, the pale skin, the tight

apple-sized perfect breasts, the fuzz of red between her legs. He was utterly transfixed, freed only when he encountered the silent plea in her eyes.

CHAPTER TEN

KATE'S BREASTS QUIVERED with each shallow breath as she watched Marco rip off his clothes, revealing his bronzed chest but taking longer to release his erection from his shorts.

She stared, the fist low in her belly tightening. She was utterly consumed by a primitive hunger, a need she had no words to express. He was quite simply beautiful. A perfect classical statue brought to warm, wonderful glowing life, each muscle perfectly defined under a warm wonderful skin.

He joined her then, arranging his long length beside her before pulling her to him. The first skin-to-skin contact drew a low keening cry from her throat.

Her back arched as his tongue slid between her parted lips while one hand moved in delicate arabesques down her back along the ridges of her spine, the other kneading the tender flesh of one breast before his mouth replaced it.

She touched him, no science or finesse to her actions, just feverish hunger for his body and an endless fascination as her hands lowered.

He pulled in a hard breath as her fingers curled around his erection, tightening around him. He stroked her arms, a feather-light touch all the way up to her chin as he found her lips. The whispered words against her mouth, forbidden exciting words, the more so because they were in a language she didn't understand, but she didn't need to.

Throbbing, he pulled away from her touch and slid his fingers into the soft wet curls at the apex of her legs, which parted to allow him to deepen the exploration as he slid one finger into her.

'You're so tight,' he murmured as her back arched to deepen his penetration. His hand still between her legs, he reached for his trousers, digging a foil package out of the slim leather clip inside before returning to her.

His nostrils flared as he stared down into her sex-flushed face, her pleasure-glazed eyes.

'Please,' she begged.

Face taut with need, he slid on the condom with a shaking hand and parted her legs, wrapping them around him as he bent over her. She felt suspended in time as she waited and then he entered her. Her body resisted just for a fraction of a second and then it expanded to accommodate him.

Kate's eyes closed as she sank deep into herself, awareness of her own body heightened in a way she had never experienced, each nerve ending quivering as he continued to stroke to reach places she had not known existed.

The words in her ear sounded like praise and encouragement as she arched into him, her fingers sliding over the sweat-slicked muscles of his back and shoulders. He was sliding over her, her skin was as hot and damp as his with the exertion of maintaining the increasingly frantic rhythm, then everything went crazy mad, and she got whisked away by a series of deep contractions that reached her toes.

Her cry of astonished pleasure was lost in his mouth.

He lay on top of her while they both fought for breath. She missed the weight when he rolled away and lay there, one hand above his head, breathing hard.

Waiting, he rubbed the ring on his finger, knowing there was always a price to pay for the pleasure of sex. The escape from his demons was only ever temporary, guilt always found him.

When nothing happened to disturb a feeling that was as close to peace as he had experienced in a long time, he turned his head. Kate smiled at him with lips swollen from his kisses, her eyes still languid and sparkling with an uncomplicated happiness that under normal circumstances he would have thought fake, but hers wasn't.

'You look very pleased with yourself.' If some major hang-ups had kept her a virgin, she was displaying no signs of them.

'I'm very pleased with you... That was... Thank you. I really didn't know it could be like that.'

'You gave yourself to me... I was your first.' It was a precious gift that he was not deserving of, but had he been offered it again, knowing what a mind-blowing experience it would be, he doubted he would have refused it.

'Mm, I suppose that does seem a bit weird. I didn't set out to stay a virgin, it's not some life choice,' she promised him earnestly. 'It just never happened, and I always thought I wasn't very...you know, I was a bit of a cold fish.'

If she had met Marco when she was eighteen there would have been no waiting.

'I have a very low opinion of the men in your life, *cara*,' he said, sounding justifiably smug.

'Not them, me,' she said, her face serious. 'I have had a…' Her nose wrinkled. 'A *tick-box* attitude to life. That probably sounds stupid, but I never realised that you can't score everything safe or unsafe, right or wrong. Some things are wrong on so many levels but yet they are marvellously, gloriously right!' Her face melted into a smile. 'I feel quite liberated.' *Also sad.* Not that she would let it spoil this moment, but she knew Marco's modus operandi, so she knew that it wasn't the start of anything marvellous, more a glimpse into what she could have had.

'I am wrong on so many levels?'

'Too many to count but you are so right… that was so right.'

'You know that this is just sex, Kate?'

She ignored the stab of hurt and rolled her eyes. 'You mean you're not going to marry me? Oh, I'm devastated,' she drawled, her eyes sparking with anger. Why did he have to ruin her perfect moment? 'But don't worry, I'll get my revenge by bad-mouthing you online.'

'I've annoyed you.' She really did look magnificent angry. Despite the fact the sweat of exertion had not dried on his skin, he felt a kick of lust.

'Why would that be? It's only fair, given there's only one of you, that you share your *magnificence* around, and I'm not greedy.'

A low rumble of laughter vibrated in the barrel of his chest as he went to grab for her, but she pulled away, sitting up in one energetic bound, her glorious hair falling in a fiery cloak over her shoulders, allowing a tempting peek of one tight nipple.

'Granted it's awkward, given my position here. But do you really think I need it spelling out that this was a one-night stand?'

'We could get around awkward.'

She stared down at him. 'You want to do this—' her gesture took in the tumbled bed-clothes '—again?'

'You're blushing.'

'I'm not,' she denied crossly. 'You want to have sex again? I didn't know you did again.'

His eyes glowed wickedly. 'Five minutes, maybe two, and I'll disprove that theory.'

It took a couple of seconds for his meaning to crystallise. 'Oh! You know what I mean... how many times?'

He turned his head and laughed. 'You intend keeping count with bedpost notches?'

'I meant—'

'I know what you meant and I know these things generally have a natural life span... they're self-limiting.'

'So, you want to sleep with me until *I* lose interest.'

He took the *I* on board and his eyes glittered with amusement. 'All right, my ego has been known to get ahead of me...until *you* lose interest?' For the first time it crossed his mind that she might say no.

'I'd love to do that again, but only—'

'You have conditions,' he said, sounding astonished at the role reversal.

'I don't want anyone to know. I don't want people to look at me and think the things they do about Rosa.'

'People respect—'

'To her face,' she interrupted, 'they show respect. I know what people think because,' she admitted, shamefaced, 'I did, a bit anyhow.'

He shrugged. 'So, you want to sneak around? That could work, in fact it might add a frisson.'

'I don't need a frisson. I just need you, and if *you* need a frisson, I don't want you.'

'Come here,' he growled. 'And I'll show how much I don't need a frisson.'

A bike ride with the Queen, a woman forty years her senior? Kate had assumed she could take it in her stride. It was actually a relief to fall off and be excused the rest of the ride.

Kate dabbed some antiseptic on the graze and flopped down on the sofa, happy to enjoy a little downtime. Freya was on a play date with her new little friend and she had the afternoon to herself.

In theory.

She had enjoyed about three minutes' alone time when Marco appeared, or, more correctly, exploded into the room.

'You have had an accident!' he accused, seemingly annoyed to find her with all her limbs intact and a chunk of chocolate halfway to her mouth.

'No…well, not really. I came off my bike before I actually expired from exhaustion. Your mother is a very fit lady. A few scratches is all.'

'Oh,' he said, losing some of the high-energy tension that had accompanied him into the room and looking almost self-conscious.

'I thought you had meetings all afternoon.'

'I did, I cancelled. Where is Freya?'

'A play date.'

'So, we are all alone.' He looked at her curled up like a kitten and felt the need rise up in him, the need to lose himself in her. The craving was like a flood tide rising.

The moments when it was possible to satisfy

the hunger she evoked in him were infrequent enough to frustrate him. Without realising it, he had fallen into a pattern of planning his weeks and days around moments like this, scheming, plotting to have time alone... The subterfuge had lost its appeal.

The knowledge that she was ashamed to have anyone know of their affair, that she was in some way ashamed of him, was really eating away at him.

It wasn't as if he wanted to take out a full-page ad to announce they were having sex, or shout it from the rooftops. Her obsession with secrecy was making a big thing out of something that wasn't... It was just sex.

Just sex. He recognised his rationalisation was becoming increasingly difficult to make, because this *just sex* had nothing in common with any *just sex* he had ever experienced before. With Kate he was feeling things he had never experienced before, that he had never allowed himself to feel before.

This should have been the ideal situation. Great sex, a beautiful woman who made no demands, but he wanted more. He didn't have a clue what more he wanted, but he did. There was a secret corner in his heart that craved something he refused to name, something that he felt he was close to when he was in her warm tight body, when he felt whole for the first time in his life.

He pushed away the thoughts. Need for her overwhelmed his disquiet that this was dangerous territory, an emotional minefield.

He bent over, kissing her as he slid a hand under her shirt and up over the warmth of her stomach until he found a breast. He weighed it in his palm, and stroked the peak with his thumb. It fitted perfectly in his hand.

'Did you lock the door?' she whispered, pushing her fingers into his dark hair but holding back as he bent in to claim her mouth.

They had been very careful but if she was honest the appeal of the illicit-thrill thing had worn off very quickly. Not so the great mind-blowing sex. Fear of when he would get tired of that lurked in the edges of her mind, unacknowledged but revealing itself more and more often of late.

She had taken great pains not to be seen as a royal mistress, but wasn't that what she was?

She was tired of the physical hiding, but more than that she was tired of pretending that she hadn't fallen deeply in love with Marco. She knew that the truth would end it all and she wasn't ready for that.

'What if I didn't?'

'You're angry?'

'I'm tired of this creeping around,' he flared without warning as he began prowling across the room with the leashed power of a big sleek jungle cat he made her think of.

Kate felt a nervous flutter in her stomach. Was this where it ended? She'd told herself she was ready for this moment and now it was here, she knew she wasn't. She knew she never would be. She loved him and when she lost him her life would be scarily empty.

He stopped, exhausted from fighting feelings he couldn't bring himself to acknowledge. 'Oh, hell, I'm sorry, it's been a foul day and... *Dio*, Kate, take me to bed.'

They took each other, stumbling across the sitting room, shedding clothes as they went, ending in her bed.

He watched her slide sinuously down his body, allowing her mouth and hands to drive him to the brink before he twisted her under and reversed their positions, entering her in one swift hard thrust, her body arched up under him to meet him.

A while later they lay in a tangle of sweat-slicked limbs.

I love you, she whispered in her head. Sad

beyond measure because she knew that if she spoke those words out loud, the words she ached to say, she would lose him.

Marco entered the apartment, his dark hair ruffled from the five-minute energetic kick-around with his daughter, and called out Kate's name.

There was no reply.

He knew she was here; the nursery nurse supervising Freya's play session had given out the information readily enough when he had casually asked her whereabouts.

She had complied, but behind the respectful smile he had been left with the distinct impression that the *casual* wasn't working. His brow furrowed. He knew how much Kate hated the idea of gossip but he had thought of a possible solution. He was working out the best way to sell it to Kate, who was not always taken by logic.

In fact, for someone who considered herself practically minded she positively embraced il-logic, which was fine so long as she carried on embracing him.

Marco found himself in the unique position of having nothing to compare to the sex he enjoyed with Kate, because it wasn't like any sex he'd had, and he'd thought he'd seen it all, done it all, short of falling in love.

Love was a no-go area that he had spent his entire adult life staying clear of, and now…he wasn't in *love* with Kate?

How would you know?

He laughed at the question in his head, swerving away sharply from that line of thought. The fact was he couldn't be in love because if he had been he'd be running in the opposite direction, and he wasn't. So why not enjoy what they had, explore it and not worry about labels while it lasted?

A furrow formed in his wide brow. It was lasting—was that significant? Boredom should have set in by now, but it hadn't. On the contrary, his *need*, his *appetite* for her had only increased over the weeks.

Some days he was…*counting the minutes*?

He made himself wait. Masochism or just to prove he *could*? Luckily, he was not into self-analysis, and he didn't need deprivation to up his libido. All that took was the thought of touching her glorious skin, of kissing her mouth when it tasted of him, of hearing that guttural little lost whimper in the back of her throat, of seeing the glazed heat in her eyes when she came.

The list of what turned him on was endless.

Walking towards the bedroom, shedding his jacket, he called her name again and pushed open the door. His smile immediately faded. He felt icy fingers in his belly.

'What are you doing?'

'Oh, I'm so glad you're here!' she exclaimed.

Some of the tension left his shoulders, then she turned and he saw she had been crying, before she literally hurled herself at his chest. His arms came around her as her head tucked under his chin.

'What has happened? Tell me,' he said, struggling with the surge of protectiveness that was too strong for him to deny ownership of.

She wanted to stay there for ever…feel his arms around her even if the safety was an illusion… She took a breath and eased herself free, struggling for composure as she tilted her head up to look at him. As their glances locked his hands slid down her arms before dropping away.

'I had a phone call from Jake,' she revealed quietly.

A dangerous scowl settled on his lean features. 'Your brother has upset you!'

Kate saw his dark expression and added quickly, 'No, not in that way. We have actually sort of made up. But he rang to give me bad news. Mum had a stroke, not serious apparently, transient something…but…well, it is considered a warning. I must have caused it, the worry about me and—'

'It is not *your* fault.'

Her slender shoulders lifted, and her lips twisted in anxiety. 'That's what Jake says, he said the doctor had suggested lifestyle changes because of her high blood pressure, a year ago or more, but she just laughed it off. The doctor also prescribed her medication, for her blood pressure and cholesterol, but she didn't tell anyone and she hasn't been taking them.'

'So *not* your fault, then.'

'If I'd been there, she might have told me, and I would have persuaded her.'

'Your mother is an adult, as stubborn, it seems, as her daughter, and she made a choice. Now hopefully she will make a better choice. It sounds like she has a second chance. Not everyone does.'

She gave a sniff and, tucking her hair behind her ears, stepped back, glancing towards the bed and the pile of clothes she'd been bundling into her case. 'I suppose you're right.'

'I am *always* right,' he corrected, hoping to make her laugh, or hit him… She managed a watery smile.

'So you are going home?' He was prepared for it, which didn't mean he had to like the idea. Freya would miss her, he told himself, not willing to make any further admission even to himself—especially to himself.

She nodded. 'Of course. They need me.'

It was the right thing to do, and he would not have expected otherwise of her, but there was a selfish part of him that wanted to say, *What about me? What about what I need?*

It's always about you, Marco, mocked the voice in his head.

'I will arrange—'

'Oh, it's all right. I explained the situation to Luca so that he could make arrangements for someone to stand in for me with Freya. My flight is all in hand apparently.'

He watched as she began to methodically fold items of clothing and stack them in her case. 'I wonder what the weight limit is—'

'There is no weight limit. Luca will be arranging for you to fly in one of our private jets.'

She wheeled round, astonishment written on her oval face. 'But—'

'Why did you tell Luca and not me?' That she had reached out to his assistant, albeit a very superior assistant about to be promoted to the post of their ambassador in the UK, troubled him more than he was prepared to admit.

Kate had too much on her mind to register his accusatory tone. She was trying not to think of saying goodbye to Freya. She had grown to love that child. Her eyes slid to the man she also loved... *Love crept up while I wasn't looking.* The words that had been going through her head while she packed shouted in her head. 'I didn't want to bother you.'

'Did it occur to you I'd want to be bothered?'

His tone made her turn, with a folded skirt pressed to her chest, a puzzled frown pleating her brow. 'Honestly, no, it didn't, Marco,' she said quietly, before turning back to her packing.

Presenting him her back was not accidental. She didn't want him to see or even suspect the tears pressing to be released, the emotions narrowing her throat.

She was a woman who had always prided herself on being self-sufficient and able to stand on her own feet. To admit the weakness was totally unacceptable and, besides, not an option.

Turning to Marco in moments of need was not the relationship they had. He had made no secret of the fact that he wanted sex with no complications. That involved no hand-holding, so his apparent indignation now was hard to stomach, she decided angrily. As if it weren't hard enough as it was, hiding the extent of her feelings, without him blurring the lines he himself had drawn.

She had worked hard at acceptance. It hadn't been easy for her. It would have been easy if she had allowed herself to read something that wasn't there into their intimacy—taking the shared laughter for tenderness, the mind-bending lust for love—and drift into a world where princes fell for the nanny. But in the real world the Prince was in love with his lost one true love.

Kate intended to live in the real world too, the one where you enjoyed it while it lasted and then felt sad, maybe even bereft, who knew? But it was her decision to take what was on offer and accept the consequences.

She needed his attitude like a... Her lips compressed. She didn't need it full stop!

'How long do you think you'll be gone?'

She paused. 'I'm not sure. It depends.'

She finished her packing methodically, aware of him moving around the room until she could bear it no more. 'Will you please stop pacing?'

'Will you stop messing with those clothes?'

he retorted, grabbing a silk shirt out of her hand and dropping it to the floor. It landed on his foot.

'That was childish,' she said when he ground it into the floor.

He looked at her for a long moment, his chest lifting as if the effort of forming the words were an effort akin to running a marathon.

'Are you coming back?'

The silence stretched. She could feel the pressure of it pounding in her ears. 'I don't know,' she admitted quietly.

'So you've thought about it!'

'Don't take that tone with me. I'm not one of your minions,' she snapped back, ignoring the fact she had never heard him be less than scrupulously polite to people who couldn't answer back.

'Of course I've thought about it.'

'I thought so!'

'You sound like you've caught me stealing the silver. Obviously, I've thought about it. I'm going and I don't know for how long. It's a natural break, a clean break.'

The thought of returning only to discover that he had moved on with someone else or just no longer wanted her was too horrifying to contemplate.

To simply slide back into the nanny role was not an option.

'Freya...'

'No!' She shoved her clenched hands in the pockets of her already snug-fitting jeans simply to stop herself hitting him as she advanced on him, making Marco think of a stalking feral cat, elegant and hissing. Even at that moment he could not but help appreciate the tight rounded curves of her bottom.

'Do not dare use Freya,' she hissed.

His head reared at the suggestion he would use his daughter, then he saw the tears standing out in her golden eyes and his antagonism fled, leaving behind an aching, a *bewildering* need to hold her, kiss away the tears.

'And do not try and guilt me out!' she snapped back.

'I wasn't. I was simply going to say that we both will miss you,' he said, not quite meeting her eyes. 'But if you want to go nobody is stopping you.'

She moistened her lips. How much, she wanted to yell, how much will *you* miss me?

The depressing answer was probably not much and not for long, whereas she would miss him for ever. Even thinking of it made the world lose its colour. The thought of her Marco-free sepia-tinged future.

'Well, it was going to happen some time, you said so yourself.'

'Did I?'

'Self-limiting? Natural lifespan? Should I go on?' She might have been flattered by his sudden desire to keep her with him had she not been fully aware the thing he objected to was not her going, but her going at a time that wasn't one of his choosing. When he was done with her there would be no long goodbye. She knew that Marco didn't do sentiment. He could be utterly ruthless.

'I will miss Freya too,' she said, her voice thick with emotion and unshed tears. 'I love her.'

She saw something flare in his eyes but a moment later they were shielded by his long, extravagant lashes. 'I know you do.'

'But we both know that when you...we... move on, my position here would be untenable. People know...the little looks. I walk into a room and they stop talking. They know, so it's going to happen some time.' Her shoulders lifted in a fake philosophical shrug. 'So why not now? I don't want to turn into Rosa.'

'I have no desire to move on, as you so euphemistically put it.' His slate-hard eyes held hers. 'Do you?' he challenged. 'You showed no desire to move on last night or—'

'Fine, point taken and no,' she admitted. 'But I don't want to drift into a situation where...' Frustration welled up inside her and the words burst out of her. 'I do want to move on to something...*more*...but you won't, Marco, you *can't*, not while you are in love with a ghost!' she finished breathlessly.

The breath hissed through his teeth as his jaw clenched. 'You know nothing about my wife or my marriage.' His voice, low and quivering with emotion, held more anger than a bellow of fury.

She bit hard into her quivering lower lip. 'I do not need it spelling out that I can't compete, and I don't want to!' She looked at the ring on his finger. 'I just pity the woman you do marry one day because she won't stand a chance, will she?'

He didn't deny it, why would he? He never had. He'd offered her no-strings sex and she had accepted the terms. This was always going to happen. There had always been a moment when she was going to find herself standing there saying goodbye to the man she loved. Leaving her heart behind and putting on a happy face.

To hell with happy faces, she decided, feeding her growing resentment.

'True, which is part of the reason I think...'

She looked at him blankly, jolted free of her dark self-pitying thoughts. 'You think?'

'I think why wait, to get married?'

She went quite pale with reaction as his meaning sank in. 'You're getting married—should I ask who the lucky lady is?'

'There is no one,' he said, sounding impatient. 'It will take me months to vet a candidate.'

She let out a whistling sound of mockery. 'And they say romance is dead!'

His lips thinned with annoyance at her flippancy. 'People search for love, but love causes more pain than anything else in a marriage. My mother and father were in love and look how that ended. Belle loved me and...'

'What happened to you was tragic,' she said quietly, her empathy for his pain almost unbearable. 'But you can't blame love.'

'It *happened* to Belle, not me.'

'This fixation you have on a loveless marriage to stay faithful to Belle... I don't see how it will work. What are you going to do? Get your bride to pass a lie-detector test? That was irony, by the way, not a suggestion.'

'I have no fixation. Marriage is a contract. I can get sex anywhere!' She winced and he grimaced. 'I did not mean you.'

'You didn't mean that I'm easy? You know,

Marco, not everyone in the world conflates love and sex.'

'They do, you have no idea how rare your attitude is.'

Kate could only stare. To think she had worried that he would see through her facade. 'My attitude, really?'

'Absolutely, a healthy attitude. Why look for a woman who won't fall in love when she is standing here?'

Kate resisted the temptation to look over her shoulder.

'You must see the pluses. It would be the ideal solution,' he added, warming to his theme. 'Freya loves you, we have great sex, you probably know me better than anyone...' He paused, the furrow between his dark brows deepening. Sometimes it felt as if they had known one another for years not weeks. 'And there would never be the worry that you have unrealistic expectations.'

'Like love you mean?' He acted as if he were offering her some perfect solution, not a nightmare life of lies.

Her tone made him frown. 'Don't make up your mind now. Think about it.'

'Have you any idea how much I hate your *reasonable* tone?' she asked him, delivering a rot-in-hell glare. 'I don't need time. The answer is a big fat no. I resent being considered the marriage equivalent of convenience food. What about what I want from life? I don't think love is fiction. I think it is a real, breathing reality!

'Your parents married for love. And,' she added, cutting off his interruption with a wave of her hand, 'it turned out badly. *You* married for love and it turned out tragically, but you think I should be denied that opportunity and settle—for what? *You?*'

His jaw quivered as he fought to make allowances for her attitude, her irrational response. She had just had bad news so it was probably not the best timing.

'So let's bring this spectacularly awful proposal to an end. I've made up my mind. I'm not coming back.'

His features froze over. 'If you think I'm going to beg you to stay…'

The idea had genuinely never crossed her mind. 'I think you will have forgotten I even existed before I walk, or actually *run*, through that door.'

He didn't say no so she took it as given.

'You know something, Marco, the next time you think your analytical brain is so bloody brilliant that you are tempted to believe your own PR machine, remember this—you just proposed to a woman who loves you...' She pressed her clenched fists against her chest and pushed out passionately. 'I love you, you stupid man, now get lost and think what a lucky escape you've had.'

'I don't want to go and see Grandpa, I want Kate. I miss Kate...' Freya wailed as she released her father's hand.

'I have explained that Kate has her own family and she has gone to see them.'

'Kate is my family...she is mine. Get her back for me. Has Kate gone to heaven like Mummy?'

Marco dropped to his knees beside the weeping child, his heart in bits. 'Oh, baby, no, she hasn't...she's in England.'

'You swear?' The little girl sniffed. 'Cross your heart?'

Marco solemnly did just that. 'Kate has other people in her life. We have to share the people we love sometimes.'

'I don't want to share her. I miss her! It's not the same without Kate here.'

A thousand images of Kate slid through his head. The feelings rose up in him so strongly that he forgot to breathe.

'I miss her too.' The admission came from some place deep inside him where a secret corner of his heart had always longed for all the things he had denied himself over the years. The things that Kate had given him: love and a family.

All the things he had denied himself out of fear of failing, of being hurt…like he wasn't hurting now!

'You do? Then will you bring her back, Papa?'

He nodded slowly. 'I will try.' *If I haven't left it too late?* He shook his head. He wouldn't, he couldn't, let himself believe that their moment had gone, that he had thrown away his one hope of happiness.

The thought of being alone again terrified him.

'Now you go to see Grandpa while I…' he began, his thoughts already moving ahead.

'You're going to get Kate, Papa. You won't forget?'

'I won't forget.'

Marco put his head around the door of his assistant's office where two young women and a man seated in a semi-circle around Luca were hanging on Luca's every word.

'Luca, a word.'

His assistant followed him back into the adjoining room.

'I am going to England, the Dorset house, I think. Oh, and I'm taking Freya with me, so her things will need to be packed.'

'There is a skeleton staff, but it will be... The security will need to be...' The younger man began thinking out loud, breaking off when he realised what he was doing. 'So when are you thinking of making the trip?'

'Tomorrow morning.'

The young man swallowed, but he had been working too long for the Crown Prince to make the error of saying anything along the lines of *impossible*.

'I need some information. I'll email the details over.'

'Fine, sir,' he said, walking into his office and addressing the heads that lifted at his entrance. 'Anyone with any plans for tonight, cancel.'

CHAPTER ELEVEN

KATE AND HER mum crossed the finish line hand in hand for the five-kilometre park run.

Kate, hands clenched against her thighs, fought for breath.

'I let you win,' her mum, in a similar position, claimed as she slugged down the contents of her water bottle before regressing to her maternal nagging role. 'Hydrate, Kate.'

'Whose idea was this?' Kate asked as she arranged her broken, or at least seriously bruised, body down on the grass.

'Yours.'

Kate propped her head on one arm and closed her eyes. 'And the doctor really signed off on this?'

'He *encouraged* this,' her mum retorted. 'It's important to stretch during cool down, Kate.'

Kate rolled her eyes and groaned.

'Now, where are your dad and Jake?'

'I don't care.' Despite the contention, Kate raised herself on one elbow. 'They were...'

'Kate, what's wrong?'

Kate said nothing. Either hallucination was a common by-product of Lycra and over-exertion, or the Crown Prince of Renzoi was standing there in conversation with her brother and dad. Did hallucinations laugh? Because hers were.

It didn't feel like much of a joke to Kate.

Her mum was shading her eyes and squinting. 'Who is that extraordinarily good-looking man talking to your dad and Jake?'

'That's Marco,' Kate said, in a flat, expressionless voice.

'Marco?'

'He was my...boss.'

'The Prince! My, what a coincidence. It really is a small world.'

Kate envied her mum her innocence. It was *not* a small world. It was a big, massive, diverse world, and no coincidence had brought Marco here today.

Speculating what had sent her thoughts in a dizzying spin. 'I feel sick,' she said faintly.

'I told you to take on more fluids.'

Kate gave a weak laugh.

Her mum looked stern as she stretched her quads. 'Seriously, Kate.'

'Your mother is right…it is science.'

Kate felt her eyes fill with tears. 'How is Freya?' she asked huskily.

'She is going to join us for supper.'

She stared at him and thought, *Back up there, mate.* 'I am not having supper with you.' She struggled rather inelegantly to pull herself up from her prone position. Once sitting, she drew her knees up to her chest and she glared up at him.

'Go away!'

'Kate!' Her mum sounded outraged.

'Mrs Armstrong, I am delighted to meet you.'

'Well, she's not delighted to meet you, so why don't you just push off?'

'Katherine! My daughter has not been herself, Your…'

Marco nodded. 'Actually, I have not been myself either, and it is not a bad thing.'

Her mother gave a wary smile. 'Well, I will leave you young people to…' She broke off as a person wearing a mini telephone box on his head, who appeared not to have read the *fun* part of the race, huffed past, yelling, 'Obstruction!'

'I really am not sure if that is totally in the spirit of the thing at all. Your father has my energy drink. I'll save you some.'

'God, let me die now.'

'Your mother looks well, you look less...'

'She trained. I didn't.' She gave a tremulous little sigh, hating that part of her wanting to beg him to stay, beg him never to leave her again.

But *she* had left and it was the right thing to do. The right thing felt absolutely mind-bogglingly miserable.

'What are you doing here, Marco?' she asked, rising to her full and not very impressive height. What she lacked in aches she made up for in imperious disdain, and Lycra made her feel taller.

He was impressive though, another scale of impressive—his sheer physicality made her stomach muscles lurch. She felt like a recovering addict coming face to face with her drug of choice.

'Your mother is well?'

Kate nodded.

Her mother had taken the warning to heart. She had turned into a health zealot. Kate had her every mouthful critiqued for nutritional value. She knew more about ketogenic deficit, good fats and the benefits of a Mediterranean diet, the last being the only fun part of the whole re-education process.

There had been a lot of education going on.

For the first time, Kate had pushed through her hurt and asked questions about her adoption, and then listened to the answers.

They had *intended* to tell her, they'd explained, but the perfect moment had never arrived and they had been afraid that she would feel rejected and different. Kate found she could accept they had been trying to protect her. How could she stay angry with people who loved her so much? Nobody made the right choices all the time. She had made some massive wrong choices of her own.

'Very well, thank you.' Aware that her face had to be shiny with sweat, she surreptitiously dabbed her upper lip with her sleeve and drank him in. The vibrancy of his skin, the razor-blade sharpness of his cheekbones, the silver grey of his eyes and the beautiful sexy outline of his sensual lips.

'Why are you here, Marco?'

He looked around. 'Is there somewhere a little more private we can talk?'

'No.' The last thing in the world she wanted was to be alone with Marco. It was also the thing she wanted most in the world as well.

The guarded expression in her beautiful eyes made him realise how much he had hurt her; his levels of self-disgust rose. 'Fair enough, but…' He glanced around and saw a bench set under a large horse-chestnut tree. 'Can we sit?'

He waited for her to step ahead of him and they walked across to the shady bench and sat down.

'Is Freya all right? Nothing is…'

'She misses you, but she is well. You and your parents, your brother…?'

'We have talked and it is…*better*. It's not an overnight process but we are working through it…'

And Kate had realised that to save Freya a moment's pain, a child who she had not given birth to, she would have lied her head off, that had been the game changer.

'Why are you here, Marco?' she asked, studying his face with hungry eyes, seeing the lines bracketing his mouth that seemed deeper and the dark smudges under his eyes.

'I missed you.'

She blinked. 'You did?' she said cautiously, damping down her ridiculous optimism. The last awful two weeks ought, if she had a brain cell in her head, to have killed her optimism stone dead.

'I want… Well, first I want to correct a few misconceptions. Firstly…'

'That is not necessary.' The last thing she

needed was to be told how he was right and she was wrong. 'I know you like the last word, but—'

'Stop talking!'

'What?'

'I… My marriage to Belle, it was not a great love match and I am not a tragic hero. Belle and I were… We watched our respective parents' marriages go down the drain. We made a youthful vow never to fall in love.' He shook his head at the memory. 'We were friends. I cared for her, valued her as a friend.'

'How is that possible? Everyone says that…?'

He saw her shiver and slid off the jacket he was wearing, draping it over her shoulders. 'You need to keep your muscles warm.'

She wasn't cold, but she liked the second-hand warmth of his skin in the fabric and the smell of his signature fragrance. 'But I thought—People say—'

'I know what people say,' he cut in with a cynical smile. 'We had the perfect marriage, never a cross word…?'

She nodded.

'No expectations, no disappointments, that was what our marriage was meant to be about, but Belle did love me. I think there were clues, but I didn't see them, didn't want to.

'I loved her, but I was not *in* love with her.

And I hurt her, she was my dearest friend, the mother of my child and I hurt her.'

'Oh, Marco!'

'Belle married me, believing she could make me love her. She got pregnant because she thought a baby, an heir would… But I couldn't love her. I didn't think I could love anyone.

'At the end, she was too ill to even hold Freya. There was… It was chaos.' He closed his eyes to blank the images playing in his head. 'She would have grown to love Freya so much. I know she would.'

Kate caught his hand, took it between both of hers and raised it to her lips. 'Of course she would.'

'One day Freya will know that I killed her mother and—'

'No!' Kate shuffled along the bench, moving in close so that his free arm automatically went around her, pulling her into his side.

'You didn't kill her, Marco.' She turned and caught his beloved face between her hands. 'Or you would be banged up in jail,' she told him bluntly. 'What happened was a tragic accident.'

He shook his head, hugging her so close that she struggled to breathe and not even seeming to be aware of it. 'She got pregnant because she thought that's what I wanted. If she hadn't… well, she'd still be here. I was the catalyst and if I had paused to see that being what was convenient for me, I... None of this would have happened if I had noticed she was unhappy.'

The self-loathing in his voice made her heart ache.

'It's crazy to blame yourself, as crazy as your father-in-law blaming Freya. Bad things happen. You can't spend the rest of your life wearing a hair shirt, you're alive,' she said, pressing a hand to his chest, feeling his heart beat beneath her fingertips. 'And Freya is alive.'

'I love Freya.'

'I know you do,' she said, her eyes warm and loving on his face. She caught his hand between her own and froze as she let it go. 'You're not wearing your ring?'

He shook his head. 'I wore it to remind me that I didn't deserve to be happy, that I didn't deserve Freya's love, and then you...' He framed her face between his big hands and took a deep breath, looking like a man who was building himself up to take a leap into the unknown... Kate watched him, her heart thudding hard against her ribcage.

'A word not spoken can change the course of your life. There is a word I have not allowed myself to speak or hear or even believe existed... Has my moment gone?'

The agonised expression on his face bewildered and alarmed her. 'It depends on what the word is.'

'Love. You are exasperating, beautiful, you swept into my life, changing it…me…for ever… I love you, Kate,' he said, giving voice finally to the words that he'd held in his heart. 'I cannot believe that I let you go because I was too much of a coward to speak. Is there any possibility that you still feel something for me…?'

A slow smile spread across her face. For Marco it was like the sun coming out.

She gave a crooked little smile the tears streaming down her face. 'I love you, Marco!' she cried joyously. 'You have no idea. I've missed you so much and…is this real?'

The kiss that went on and on proved that it was very real indeed.

'Coming up for air any time soon?'

Kate pulled away, though not too far, clinging to Marco as if she were afraid he'd vanish. 'Oh, Jake—this is Jake, my brother. Jake, this is Marco, my—'

'Future husband,' Marco inserted, nodding to Kate's brother. 'We have met.'

'Future husband…married? Should you not ask me first?'

'I'm asking you now.'

'In that case, yes, please.'

'Shall I go away?' Jake asked, and did, but the couple wrapped in each other's arms didn't notice.

EPILOGUE

KATE TWISTED TO get a look and see if the stand-up pearl-encrusted collar that framed her face was lying properly, high in the front, the contrasting low vee neckline at the back revealing the delicacy of her shoulder blades.

She had requested nothing that resembled a meringue and no train. The first wish had been granted—her dress was a column that spilled like a pool of warm ice at her feet.

The clever design made her feel taller and the ivory silk, one shade up on the colour chart than her skin tones, made her skin glow like a pearl.

Allowing for artistic over statement, Kate was happy with the results. She had a train, but it was short, and encrusted with pearls and finely embroidered wrens, which were the symbol of Renzoi.

'You look beautiful.'

She turned to find Marco looking gorgeous in black denim and an open-necked shirt, standing watching her, a half-smile on his face.

'It's unlucky to see the bride in her dress before the wedding,' she reproached sternly.

'We're already married, *cara*, and I'm happy to break tradition.'

Her expression softened into goofy adoration. 'Not technically.'

There had been no celebrant, but the vows they had exchanged in front of their family, Kate carrying a posy of daisies, and a few close friends in Dorset the previous week had been for them a special thing. It might have no legal standing that would come with the pomp and circumstance of the full bells-and-whistles royal wedding tomorrow, but they had considered themselves bonded for life from that moment.

'Thank you for doing that for me.' The royal wedding had not been optional, but Marco had known how much she was dreading it and had arranged, with the help of her mum, something that was just for her. The wild flowers in jam jars decorating the tables had been the thoughtful contribution of Lady Rosa, and the tandem with the big shiny bell was the

Queen's gift, along with a new bicycle for the bridesmaid, their daughter.

'I was checking it still fits.' She pressed a hand to her stomach.

'And does it?'

She nodded. 'I won't show for ages yet.'

'Our secret. I like that. Keep the world out for as long as possible, or as long as Kate cannot blurt it out to everyone.'

'It still doesn't feel real. I don't know how it happened.'

His lips twitched. 'I think you should consider a planned caesarean.'

She pressed a finger to his lips. 'Let's just relax and enjoy this, take one step at a time and take medical advice…?'

He forced a smile. 'You're right.' His glance shifted to the box on the bed. 'Have you decided?'

Her mum had given her the box that contained everything she knew about Kate's birth parents she possessed.

She had handed a similar one to Jake and his search had not ended happily. Kate knew the same might happen to her.

'I'll open it now. Will you stay?'

'Of course, *cara*.'

He watched as Kate in her silk dress opened the lid as if all Pandora's secrets were about to rush out.

'There's not much here,' she said, picking up the few papers that were in it. A photo fluttered out from between the brown-edged papers.

Kate lifted it up, her eyes wide as she studied it.

'What is it? What is wrong?'

She handed him the photo of two babies.

'I think I have a twin, Marco, an identical twin.'

'Do you want to find her?'

'I don't know. I really don't know.'

'Well, when you decide I will be here for you, supporting you, you know that.'

Kate smiled and as always it took his breath away. 'I know that, and I hope my sister, wherever she is, has been as lucky as I am. Hold me, Marco.'

He did, and Kate knew that whatever happened, whatever decision she made, she was safe and loved.

* * * * *

Were you enchanted by
The Prince's Forbidden Cinderella?
*Then why not dive into
these other dazzling stories
by Kim Lawrence?*

Claiming His Unknown Son
Waking Up in His Royal Bed
The Italian's Bride on Paper
Innocent in the Sicilian's Palazzo
Claimed by Her Greek Boss

Available now!